Free Winds Blow West

Center Point
Large Print

Also by L. P. Holmes and available from
Center Point Large Print:

The Crimson Hills

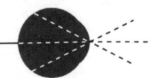

**This Large Print Book carries the
Seal of Approval of N.A.V.H.**

Free Winds Blow West

L. P. HOLMES

CENTER POINT LARGE PRINT
THORNDIKE, MAINE

Printed in the United States of America
on permanent paper.
Set in 16-point Times New Roman type.

ISBN: 978-1-62899-976-1

Library of Congress Cataloging-in-Publication Data

Names: Holmes, L. P. (Llewellyn Perry), 1895–1988, author.
Title: Free winds blow west / L. P. Holmes.
Description: First edition. | Thorndike, Maine : Center Point Large Print,
2016. | ©2016 | Series: A Circle V Western
Identifiers: LCCN 2015051005 | ISBN 9781628999761
    (hardcover : alk. paper)
Subjects: LCSH: Large type books. | GSAFD: Western stories.
Classification: LCC PS3515.O4448 F74 2016 | DDC 813/.52—dc23
LC record available at http://lccn.loc.gov/2015051005

Chapter One

He came down across the looping foothills of the Lodestone Mountains, letting his long-striding black horse set its own pace along the cattle trails that followed this little watercourse fringed by alders and willows. Yesterday afternoon he had struck the headwaters of the creek, and last night he had made his frugal camp beside its chuckling waters. Today, keeping to the winding run of it, he had begun passing cattle—stocky whitefaces bearing a Rocking A brand. He flushed them from favored watering spots and saw others bunched in little meadows that broke and widened here and there. Knowing cattle, he sensed in them more than a natural wariness. They were fretful and uneasy, a condition of things that he turned over in his mind and at which he wondered.

He sat tall in the saddle, for he was long-bodied and sinewy, and solid through the shoulders. His deeply weathered features were lean, flat of jaw, and his chin was hard angled. The faint line of an ancient scar angled across one solid cheek bone. Pressure at the corners thinned his lips slightly, touching his mouth with a habitual grimness. There was a trick of erectness in the cast of his head that gave his gray-eyed glance a certain penetrating intentness. There was about him a physical and mental competence, a bold, tough sufficiency, alert yet taciturn. Bruce Martell was a man who rode alone, liked it so, and who neither asked nor gave odds.

His jeans and jumper and gray flannel shirt were well worn, but showed a certain neatness in fit and appearance, the apparel of a man staunch in his own self-respect. His riding gear held the same plain, but well-cared-for and good quality look. His spur rowels had been filed down to blunted stubs, in definite regard for the horse under him. A rifle in a scabbard was slung under his near stirrup leather and the holstered gun belted about his saddle-leaned waist was as plain and business-like as the rest of his outfit.

Here the trail turned and dipped, crossing a sparkling shallows of the creek, and the hoofs of the black horse beat up a faint spray that was cool fragrance in a land whipped to tawny dryness by the solid beat of a late-summer sun. There was a long thicket of scrub willow through which the trail dodged and ducked before breaking into still another meadow, and at the lower end of this there was sudden movement that pointed and held Martell's glance.

A single slinking coyote was of small consequence, but when a man glimpsed a full half dozen of these wary scavengers, scuttling away through the alders and willow patches, he was faced with a possible significance he could not afford to ignore. So now Martell drew the black to a halt and let the careful survey of his glance run out ahead. The coyotes almost instantly vanished, but there, beyond a fringe of willows, lifted a fairly lofty alder tree, and in the branches of this several buzzards perched like somber-robed ghouls, craning naked necks as they watched rider and horse fixedly.

There was a faint stir of breeze pushing up the creek and with crinkled nostrils Martell tested it, found it fresh and clean, carrying no taint of carrion. He put the black horse to movement again, drifting down the meadow. At this closer approach the buzzards lifted from the alder with heavy flapping, then soared in wheeling, dipping circles, heads cocked as they watched with black, beady eyes.

Martell's horse laid the broad of its chest against a final barrier of willow and broke through into a little glade beyond, where, plain to the eye, were scattered the reason and cause of this gathering of furred and feathered scavengers. The remains of four beef carcasses cluttered the glade.

Martell pulled up. The story was plain enough. Not too many hours before—yesterday afternoon or evening perhaps—these cattle had been butchered, hurriedly and wastefully. Only the loins and haunches had been taken, the balance left to the blowflies, the buzzards, and coyotes. Decomposition had not yet fully set in.

This, mused Martell, was slow-elking if he'd ever seen it. Any cow outfit, butchering beef for its own legitimate use, would not have killed four animals at once, nor would they have left so much good meat go to waste.

Considering the matter, Martell thumbed tobacco sack and paper from a pocket of his jumper and spun a cigarette into shape. It was while he was busy at this that the black horse swung an alert head, ears pricked. At the same instant Martell heard the muffled thump of hoofs, coming up along the creek. And then there was a voice calling, harsh and dominant.

"The buzzards lifted out of that tallest alder, just ahead. We'll have a look around there."

Martell straightened slightly in his saddle, swung the black around so that it put his right side to the downstream approach. He lit his cigarette, alertness a cold spark in his eyes. They understood each other, Martell and his horse, for now, under the caressing pressure of its rider's hand, the big, black gelding turned motionless as a statue, waiting out those approaching hoofs.

Four riders broke through the willows at the lower end of the glade. At what they saw before them, they pulled in abruptly, and from the lips of their leader, a spare, leathery-faced man with a nearly white, sickle mustache that framed a grim, bear-trap mouth, burst words of bitter anger.

"Knew it! Knew we'd find something like this.

Those damned settlers . . . so smug and self-righteous! More of the same old thievery. Four good ones this time . . . slow-elked!"

The torrent of the speaker's anger broke off abruptly as his furious glance, sweeping the glade, came to rest on Martell and the statue-like black. For a moment he stared, then growled with savage authority.

"Watch him, boys! Carp, come up with me!"

They came spurring up, this older man and one who was younger and burly through the shoulders, with a thick neck and a ruddy intolerance all across a broad and blocky face. They set to a skidding halt in front of Martell and the impact of their eyes was a hot, suspicious challenge. The older man's voice was like a whiplash.

"What d'you know about this?"

Martell shrugged. "Not a thing, except that you are plainly right in calling it slow-elking. I got here only a couple of minutes before you rode in."

"You're from where and going where?"

This time it was no shrug that caused Martell's shoulders to swing restlessly. And his eyes darkened slightly, as though brushed over with smoke. He jabbed a back-pointing thumb over his shoulder and a stabbing index finger ahead.

"From there . . . to there."

"Not definite enough . . . not by a hell of a ways. What's your business around here?"

It was the younger, burly-shouldered one who

threw this blunt statement and question and the hot intolerance of him burned in his words.

Now the smoke did gather in Bruce Martell's eyes and his tone, drawling before, turned brittle.

"Let's ease up on the reins a mite. You"—he looked at the older man—"got a right to be warmed up, if, as I figure, you owned this beef. Only, don't jump at conclusions. But you"—and here Martell switched his glance to the burly rider—"where I'm heading for, and why, is none of your damned affair. Do I make myself clear?"

The burly one flushed angrily, leaned forward in his saddle. The older man snapped a harsh command.

"Easy does it, Carp. Let me handle this."

He made another hard, searching appraisal of Bruce Martell.

"Yeah," he said. "I owned those steers. I'm Hack Asbell and the Rocking A is my iron. What you see here ain't the first I've lost. This sort of thing has been going on ever since the first rush of sod-busters hit Indio Basin. They seem to think that Rocking A beef is God's free gift to the hungry. It ain't. And somebody is due to damned well find that out, even if it takes a rope and a tall tree to convince 'em."

Martell nodded. "Cattle stealing is cattle stealing, slow-elking being part of it. It'd be bad enough if they took the whole carcass, but to take just the loins and quarters and leave the rest to rot, that's worse than bad, and I savvy just how you feel about it. In your place I'd feel the same. Yet I say again, that I know nothing about this. I came across the Lodestones and you can follow my back trail to prove it, if you're of a mind to."

The hot, fuming intolerance in Carp Bastion was too much for him to hold back. He rolled his burly shoulders forward almost as if throwing a blow.

"That's what you say. Nobody ever seems to know anything about this damned thieving business. Still it goes on. You could be lying, just like all the rest of them. I think so."

Martell's look went bleakly harsh. The pressure of his knee sent the black horse lunging forward. It crashed into Carp Bastion's mount, nearly upsetting the animal. Martell's reaching hand locked in the front of Bastion's shirt and with one lifting, savage jerk he hauled his man out of the saddle and flung him smashing facedown to the hard earth. Then Martell was backing his horse away, his spread right hand flat against his thigh, close to his holstered gun.

"Mister," he rapped coldly, "you talk too damned much."

There was a hard yell of anger and the two riders at the lower end of the glade came spurring up. A gusty rashness ruffled Martell's cheeks and the swing of his glance missed no move on the part of any of them.

"When a man calls me a liar, he's pushed his jaw too far," he warned. "Don't get rough. Numbers don't necessarily mean a damned thing."

Hack Asbell had come up the hard way in a tough and wild land. He knew a dangerous man when he saw one and he knew he was looking at one now. His voice whipped his men back.

"Cut it fine, boys. Carp more or less asked for that." He fixed bleak eyes on Martell, then jerked his head. "This creek leads to the Hayfork River. The river is my line. Get across it and stay across. I'm giving you the benefit of the doubt . . . this time."

Carp Bastion's headlong collision with the earth had done his face little good. His chin was skinned, his lips split, and blood was seeping from his nose. He was dazed and he was raging. He tried to get up, but fell over on his side and in that position was pawing clumsily and blindly for his gun.

"Hold him down!" rapped Martell. "If this thing goes any further, it'll be because he won't learn."

One of the other riders flashed from his saddle, grabbed Bastion's gun, and took it away from him. Martell looked at Hack Asbell.

"The name is Bruce Martell. I expect to be around Indio Basin for a time. I don't like slow-elkers any better than you do. Should I run across any trail of them, I'll let you know. Sorry this affair had to turn a little rough."

He swung the black and loped down the glade, smashed through the willows below, and was gone.

Carp Bastion finally found his feet and lurched blindly toward his horse.

"I'll kill him!" he blurted thickly. "I'll ride him down and . . . !"

"You'll shut up and cool off and stay right where you are!" cut in Hack Asbell harshly. "I'm thinking we both made damn' fools of ourselves. That fellow was giving it to us straight. And one thing is certain. You'll never meet up with a tougher, more dangerous man. We'll be getting along home. We're too late to do any good here and I sure ain't enjoying myself looking at what's scattered around this glade."

"Mebbe if we work from here, we'll pick up a trail, boss," suggested one of the other riders.

Hack Asbell shrugged. "And if we did . . . what?" he growled bitterly. "It would just lead into the basin, like all the rest of the trails we've followed. And there it would break up and scatter and we'd end up chasing our tails, same as usual. It's one thing to accuse a dozen men. It's something else trying to accuse five hundred. No, what we've got to do is ride earlier and later and farther. We've got to catch these damn' slow-elkers cold . . . in the act or with the meat. Then we can really do something about it. Come on. Let's get out of here."

Chapter Two

Indio Basin was a land of rolling distances and the afternoon was well along by the time Bruce Martell rode into Starlight, a town set down here in the heart of the basin. It had started as a stage station, lonely and with little hope of real permanence. Then a gradual increase in trade and income from scattered cattle outfits had given it added substance and some growth. And so it had remained, a weather-stained little wilderness cattle town until the wild stampede of the present had caught it up, engulfed it, and left it as it was now, wild-eyed, bewildered, and bursting at the seams, growing madly overnight without plan or reason or law.

Government land, the wide miles of Indio Basin had been. Cattle outfits, grazing their herds upon it, knew this and, with one exception, drugged themselves with the high optimism that it was a condition that would continue to exist, time without end. The lone exception was Hack Asbell. While content and hoping for unruffled continuance of the *status quo*, Asbell was shrewd enough to realize that the odds were all the other way, and so he had prepared for what was now taking place. Retreating north of the Hayfork River, Asbell had settled on, filed on, and acquired enough range to establish a permanent head-quarters that gave him access to all the foothill country of the Lodestones, land that he knew would never appeal to the vast run of settlers. From here he had continued to operate, grazing on basin grass south of the river, until word of the poised land rush came down across the miles. Then he had drifted his cattle back across the river and into the foothills.

Other outfits, less long-headed, on getting the word that the government was opening Indio Basin to settlement, ranted and raved, cursed and threatened, but got nowhere against stern-talking government agents sent in ahead to ready things for the poised tide. Their day in Indio Basin was done and in their hearts they knew it; so finally, with a vast reluctance, they began moving out, most of them driving south into the broken country beyond the distant Selkirks.

And so, on the great day, from the jump-off point along War Lance Creek, away out to the east, the land rush had poured, and in short weeks had spread settlers and their wagons over the basin's sun-whipped distances.

Coming into this town of Starlight, Bruce Martell told himself that it was the wagon that was the real identification of the settler. Starlight was jammed with them—wagons lurching and rumbling into town, wagons lurching and rumbling out again, new wagons and old ones, sound ones and rickety ones, ponderous freighters, canvas-topped Conestogas, spring wagons, buckboards, buggies, carts. The single, steadily lengthening street was one mad tangle of them and the dust of that street, never having a chance to settle, hung in a constant shroud over everything, an amber mist, shot through with the afternoon sunshine. Wagons—wagons—and people.

The crush of activity was greatest around the door of a building that carried a newly painted sign across its front:

Land Office
Cashel Edmunds, Agent

Here men sweat and swore, milled and pushed and argued, trying to get into the place, trying to get out of it. Tempers were short. Two men, jostling each other for space, suddenly began swinging their fists. They were elbowed aside and left to fight it out, the rest paying them no attention. The drive of more important things was at hand. Even the two battlers suddenly realized this, for they broke off their brawling, looked around foolishly, then renewed their efforts to get into the Land Office.

Bruce Martell had thought of trying the Land Office for the information he was seeking, but sight of this struggling mob decided him against it. He saw he'd be hours getting into the place and waiting his turn, with the chances better than even that he wouldn't then find out what he wanted to know.

Martell had expected a lot of settlers in Indio Basin, but nothing like the actuality. Where he'd expected scores, there were hundreds. All the way in from Hayfork River he'd passed their camps, some already settled on the piece of land of their choice, while many more, late-comers, were scurrying every which way, seeking a parcel of land not already claimed—and having no great amount of luck at it.

Some had merely set their wagons down in the middle of their quarter-section, made frugal camp, and seemed to be resting up after the rigors of the rush, while others, more industrious and of greater energy, were already at work, marking out foundations of the homes they hoped to build, laying out the lines of fields they hoped to plant. One settler, Martell had seen, was already following a plow, breaking the virgin summer-hardened sod in one thin furrow all along his line, believing perhaps that this would prove an inviolate badge of ownership and so hold back any and all encroaching claims.

At several camps along the way, Martell had stopped to ask his question. At none of them had he been received even civilly, let alone being given any information. From one camp a surly growl followed him:

"Damned cowhand! Wouldn't tell him, even if I knew!"

And that, Martell had mused, was the way it had always been and would always be. There was no common ground on which a man of the saddle and a man of the plow could ever meet, it seemed. Always there were suspicions and hatreds and deep-running enmity.

Even here in Starlight, for all their rush and frenzy, the settlers found time to show how they felt toward any man of the saddle with the look of cow country about him. Several times, as he worked his horse slowly along the street through the crush of wagons and scurrying humans, Martell knew the impact of this ancient and deep-seated animosity. Antagonistic growls and plenty of muttered curses were thrown his way, and once the lash of a long whip cracked like a pistol shot, only inches from his face.

He had ignored the verbal abuse, realizing it was as useless to try and silence it as it was to still the buzzing of a swarm of bees. But that whistling whiplash was something else again. It had been done with deliberate intent and, had it landed fairly, could have cut his face to the bone. So he twisted abruptly in his saddle, dark anger running all through him, thinning his lips, smoking up his eyes, but he had had no luck in locating the source of the taunting lash, for wagons were jammed all about him and the whip could have reached for him from any one of a half dozen jeering, mocking drivers. There was nothing to do but work the black out of the crush and think things over.

Bruce Martell was no trouble hunter. He was a tough, capable man, full of quiet, steely pride, but insofar as events would allow, he governed himself and his actions with more than an ordinary amount of prudence and common sense. To him, a trouble hunter or a troublemaker was about as obnoxious a specimen as there was, and he had no patience with one. Only a fool asked for trouble when he could avoid it with dignity and the full retention of his own self-respect.

Yet he knew the limits of his own temper and he realized that, if he continued to ride through this town and any more whiplashes came his way, anything might happen. Prudence suggested that he get out of the saddle and go about his business on foot, where he would be less conspicuous.

There was a big general store directly across the street from the Land Office and, though the hitch rail in front of it was jammed hub to hub with wagons of all sorts and the low, long porch crowded with people, when he reined the black around to the rear of the place, he found himself comfortably free of the rush and turmoil. Here was a sprawling freight corral, holding a number of horses, with a pair of big Merivale freighters standing, high and empty, to one side. He tethered the black to a corral rail, then went around on foot to try his luck in the store. Perhaps a question or two here might help.

Again he was doomed to disappointment. While he did manage to get inside the door of the place, the space between him and the counter was jammed with settlers and their women, all clamoring at once for the attention of the two harried, sweating men behind the counter. Martell saw this was neither the time nor place to get what he wanted.

He was turning back to the door when a shift of the close-packed crowd brought someone stumbling against him. The end of a fifty-pound sack of flour jammed into his chest, then thumped to the floor at his feet. A soft cry of feminine dismay sounded.

"Oh . . . I'm sorry! I didn't mean to . . . but it was pretty heavy, and it was a case of drop the flour or fall down myself. Please . . . I'm really sorry . . . !"

Martell's first thought was that her hair was almost the exact shade of rich russet that touched aspen leaves on the high summits after the first frost. Her blue eyes were wide and very clear and her lips were a crimson curve of consternation. She was slim and supple and strong, but a fifty-pound sack of flour was a full-size tussle for a person like her under the best of circumstances, let alone in this jostling, pushing, heedless crowd.

The sternness of Martell's lips broke into a faint smile that softened his face amazingly.

"Lady," he said, "think nothing of it. Anything might happen in a stampede like this." He caught up the sack of flour, shouldered it. "Now if you'll show me where to take it . . . ?"

He liked her quick common sense. She wasted no time in empty protest. The curve of her lips became an answering smile. "Thank you. You're very kind. This way."

She moved ahead of him through the crowd, out of the hectic doorway. Her shoulders were straight and gracefully square and the heavy luxury of her hair lay in a thick roll at the nape of her slender neck. There was a spring wagon with its team of shaggy broncos tied at the hitch rail at the far end of the store porch and here the girl paused.

"In here," she said. "Thank heavens! That's the heavy part of the chore done with. Now to go back into that madhouse and battle for the rest of it."

Martell dumped the sack of flour into the back of the spring wagon and brushed the worst of its snowy dust from his jumper. "If you need any more help . . . ?" he drawled.

She shook her ruddy head. "I can handle what's left. Thank you again."

She turned and hurried away, and Martell watched her until she had worked a way into the store again. Then, with a shrug and another faintly

21

fleeting smile in tribute to the first pleasant interlude this country had afforded him, he turned to renewed consideration of his own problems.

Next door to the store was a saloon, doors winnowing steadily. A sign, angling across the front, named the place as THE FRONTIER. The saloon, Martell knew, would be just as jammed as the rest of the town. But men would be having their drinks and moving on about their affairs, so in all probability he could find a niche at the bar and ask his questions while waiting for his drink. He moved over to the doors and went in.

Here as he expected was more of the crowd of pushing restless humans. Men elbowed a way to the bar, yelled and argued for service, and, when they finally got it, drank thirstily and went out again, with more always clamoring to take their places. Only the shadowy gloom of the place gave any suggestion of coolness.

In time Martell reached the bar, threw down a coin, and had a bottle of warm beer thrust at him by one of three perspiring bartenders.

"A moment, friend," said Martell. "I'm looking for a settler by the name of Clebourne . . . Jeff Clebourne. Would you by chance have heard the name or have any idea what section of the basin he filed on?"

The bartender paused only to scrub the sweat from his face with the tail of his bedraggled apron. "Mister," he answered heavily, "I don't know anybody's name or where anybody's filed. If this damn' rush don't slow up pretty quick, I won't even know my own name. Sorry." He hurried away, answering the clamoring desires of others along the bar.

Martell drank his beer slowly. All he could say for it was that it was wet and that it cut the dust from his throat. He thought again of the letter he'd received from his younger brother Kip. He wished Kip had been a little more explicit in his directions. Yet, on second thought, the chances were that at the time the kid had no idea himself as to just where in Indio Basin Jeff Clebourne would finally stop his wagons and set up his boundary stakes. That he'd eventually come up with the Clebourne layout, Martell was confident. It was just a case of ride and look until finally, somewhere, he'd either get a lead by word of mouth, or stumble across the camp itself. But the chore, with conditions as confused as they were all across these wide miles, wasn't looking any the less difficult. Martell tipped his head back, drained the last mouthful from his bottle. At that moment a hard elbow drove into his ribs and a voice grated mockingly.

"Move along, cow wrastler! This ain't your country any more. Move along . . . and make room for a better man!"

Martell turned, putting the broad of his shoulders against the bar. Facing him was a

23

tall, sloppily lank individual with a face that was narrow and bony, with eyes little and evil and deep-set, and a loose mouth. Behind the man stood two others of much the same mold and look. It had been a fairly tough day. The weariness of long miles in the saddle pulled at Martell's muscles. Plain physical hunger was a living thing in his vitals. All day long he had met with scarcely a single civil word or gesture of good will. There had been that ruckus back in the foothills of the Lodestones at the scene of the slow-elking, and after that was the surly hostility he'd met in all the scattered settler camps along the trail. Still rankling at the back of his mind was the memory of curses and growls and jeers from men on foot and men on high wagon boxes. Finally there had been the slashing snap of that whiplash, barely missing his face. Now, here was still further affront, deliberate and calculated in its intent, from still another of this damned mob of stamping, cursing, heedless settlers.

The temper that had burned in Martell several times before throughout the day once more surged at the barrier of his self-restraint, sending the fluttering of raw tension across his cheeks, flattening the corners of his lips, darkening his eyes, and bringing him up and poised on his toes. But he fought it back, in part at least. His voice ran, low and somewhat toneless. "At another time and place, mister, you'd have bought yourself a chore of proof. About being a better man, I mean."

He would have turned away with that, but he wasn't to get off so easily. This lank brute in front of him had sought this thing deliberately, recognizing a lone saddle man in hostile company. The jamming numbers of his own kind about him filled the fellow with confidence. "You move too slow, cow wrastler," he leered. "Get goin'!"

He reached out, gave Martell a violent shove. Martell's temper turned to cold rage and spilled over. Reckless of consequence, he twisted the empty beer bottle and smashed it fully into the narrow, jeering face. It was a wicked blow, wickedly meant. The bottle crashed to fragments and the man went down.

There were many in this close-packed room who neither saw nor heard any part of the start of this thing, so close was the crush, so steady and raucous the din of men's voices. But from those immediately around Martell, a concerted growl arose, along with a swift-building physical pressure as they began closing in on him. Instantly Martell realized that he was in for something that could be very bad. Conceivably he might be lucky to get out of this thing alive.

Chapter Three

The two who had stood behind the man Martell clubbed down gave back slightly at the blow. Then they came lunging in together and in the whipping hand of one of them gleamed the bared steel of a knife.

Martell had no chance to go for his gun; they were too close to him. He threw up his left arm as a barrier against that driving knife and felt the slide of steel across the heavy muscles just below the point of his shoulder, and the keen edge of the weapon burned like a white-hot iron. The fellow behind the knife, carried forward by the violence of his deadly lunge, was wide open to the blow Martell smashed at his body. Martell put everything he had into the punch, for he knew he could not risk another drive from that knife.

He felt the fellow's belly muscles cave under his knuckles, heard the eruptive gasp of agony. The knife wielder sagged to his knees, retching and sick. Martell kicked him in the face, then went right over him after the third of this trouble-hunting trio.

They met, chest to chest, and the settler was like some mad, crazy animal. He clawed, stamped, gouged, tried to jam Martell back against the bar and corner him there. Keeping his hands low, Martell took two mauling blows in the face before he could smash his man twice in the midriff. This gained him room enough to straighten and hammer a solid one home to the snarling face. The fellow went back, floundering, and Martell seized on this respite to break away from the bar and drive into the crowd toward the door.

It was heavy going. They came at him from all sides, aiming wild, clubbing blows, trying to beat him down. But the very weight of their own numbers partially defeated this purpose, for in the mad crush none could get a clear smash at him. It became a struggling, no-quarter, cursing bedlam, a whirlpool of savage humanity, with Bruce Martell in the vortex.

Martell took blows. He was bound to, what with the number being thrown at him. Fists bounced off his head and face, bloodied his mouth. They hurt him and shook him up, but they were not too damaging. He did not make the mistake of trying to answer too many of them. Instead, throwing the full weight of his shoulders and all the driving strength in his back and legs into the effort, he bulled his way doggedly along.

A chair was trampled underfoot, splintered. A poker table skidded back and forth before the whirling drive of bodies. A hulking settler, cursing it as an obstruction, grabbed the edge of the table and upset it, and it immediately became something for men to become entangled with and to fall over.

Martell stumbled over one leg of it himself, but managed to keep his feet. A settler, who had just nailed Martell with the hardest blow he'd yet felt, tangled with the same obstruction and reeled off balance, arms waving wildly. Martell paid him back, hitting him with the full roll of his shoulders behind the punch, and the settler went headlong.

That upturned table became an ally of Martell's. He was past it now, but those after him tripped and staggered, went down, dragging others with them. And now Martell reached the far wall, beside the door. He put the flat of his shoulders against this secure barrier and, for the moment, found things slightly clear before him. He jammed his right hand down, found his gun still in the holster, drew it, and drove one booming shot into the floor.

"Give way!" he panted hoarsely. "Get back! I'll kill the next man who tries to lay a hand on me. Back up, damn you . . . back up!"

They gave way. The lusting fury of the mob was not enough to blind them to the potent threat of that big black gun. And they saw in the dark storm in Martell's eyes, in the hard, bloodied line of his mouth, a bitter determination to do exactly as he threatened. So they crowded back and widened the cleared space before him.

He sidled along the wall, shoulders brushing it.

His knife-cut left arm was outstretched, fingers feeling the wall as he moved, but his eyes never left that bleakly hating group in front of him, nor did his ready gun waver in the slightest. Now his exploring left hand located the door post and he giving swing of the portal beyond. A quick lunge drove it open, and then he was through and into the street beyond. Clamoring like blood-hounds, the settler mob poured out after him. Martell darted into the wagon-cluttered street, barely escaped being trampled by one rearing team, then dodged to momentary safety beyond a lumbering, two-wagon freight outfit.

There ahead of him, just spinning into the clear from the hitch rail before the store, was a spring wagon behind a pair of shaggy broncos. At the reins was a slim figure with hair the color of autumn-dressed aspen leaves. She saw him on the instant, and he saw her eyes go wide and startled.

There was a quick mind under that crown of shining hair. She seemed to see and understand all that was behind his bloodied mouth and the bleak desperation in his eyes, for she locked the brake of her wagon and set the broncos up rearing.

"Quick!" she cried. "In here!"

Martell shook his head. "Not your affair. And there could be shooting!"

A settler, faster of foot than his fellows, broke past the freight outfit, came charging. Martell dodged, cuffed him with the barrel of his gun, knocked him sprawling.

The girl's voice was a high, urgent peal. "Don't be an idiot! Quick . . . up here with me!"

With the words she reached past Martell with her whiplash, cutting across the face still another settler who had dodged past the wagon tangle. The fellow stumbled back, hands pawing his face, cursing crazily.

"Quick!" she cried once more. "It's your only chance!"

Martell grabbed at the iron seat rail, swung himself up beside her. The girl's whip came down again, this time across the bunched haunches of her team. The broncos hit their collars in a wild lunge. The wagon shot ahead.

For a hundred yards it was a wild ride. How they got through, Bruce Martell never knew. The girl's slim forearms were rigid, as, half risen from the wagon seat, she guided the plunging broncos through the tangle. The spring wagon skidded almost half around a creaking Conestoga, seemed certain about to crash into the side of it, straightened clear at the last split second. It almost miraculously dodged a ponderous freighter, took a wheel clear off a flimsy cart, letting that conveyance and its driver down in a cloud of dust and a fading howl of outraged, sulphurous cursing. They seemed inevitably trapped between two more heavy freighters, but at the last moment shot through an opening so narrow Martell distinctly heard the click of iron-rimmed wheel hubs kissing as they passed.

Beyond was reasonable space and now the broncos really flattened to their chore. Behind, the street was all a-rumble with seething, bawling anger, but this faded swiftly with distance. In a few more tense, dust-clogged moments they were beyond the limits of town and whirling away into the wide prairie ahead.

Martell twisted in the seat and looked back. He could see no sign of further pursuit forming and he doubted there would be any. This whole crazy business had been too wild and confused and spontaneous to carry much follow-through. It was like a flash fire in a thicket of dry brush, a quick, hot, towering flame, and then cooling ashes.

The temper of the settler mob wasn't deep enough to last long. It had been a rough, wicked brawl, but no one had been killed. As long as the settler mob had something immediately in front of it to hate and take a swing at, it was dangerous and lusting. But the mob wasn't up to gathering means of pursuit and leaving town and the drive of their own affairs on what could now be an empty chase. The big hate had brewed in the saloon, and there most of it would remain.

"You can slow 'em down, now," Martell told the girl. "It's all over."

She pulled the broncos to a jog, to a walk, and then to complete halt.

"I don't know why I did it," she said, her voice strained and muffled. "I heard a gunshot, just before you broke into the street. You killed somebody back there."

Martell shook his head. "No. I just shot into the floor, to make 'em back away from me."

He saw that reaction had gripped her. She was trembling, and gnawing at her lips, which were bloodless. Just a slip of a girl, but she had been magnificent. Martell told her so.

"In my time I've seen some exhibitions of cold nerve. I never saw anything to equal yours. I don't know yet how you took the rig through, ma'am."

Perhaps his words or the fervor of his tone did it. Or maybe it was the quick recovery of sturdy youth and courage. At any rate color swept back to her softly sun-tanned cheeks and the strain about her lips softened. She turned her head and the full, direct clarity of her eyes searched him.

"What was the trouble about?"

"I happen to be a saddle man," said Martell quietly, only partially covering the bitterness in his voice. "As such, every ham-footed settler I've run across seems to feel that I'm a pin game, to be cursed and snarled at and pushed around. I went into that place quietly, minding my own business, wanting only to ask a couple of questions about some people I'm trying to locate.

Some settlers started whip-sawing me and just wouldn't let me out without a fight. It was pretty rough in there." He scrubbed the back of his hand across his crimsoned lips and unconsciously lifted his left arm to look at it. Seeping blood was sliming all down across the back of his left hand.

The girl cried out softly.

"Yeah," said Martell. "I'm spilling a little blood. Not of much account. One of that settler crowd had a knife. He got a little of me, but not too deep. So now I'll thank you again and quit bothering you, ma'am. I got a horse back in town I've got to get."

He started to get out of the wagon, but the girl would have none of it. "You'll not go back! That crowd . . . they'd . . . they'd . . . !"

Martell smiled bleakly. "With a little room to move around in and a chance to watch my back, I'm not afraid of that gang. And I can't leave my bronc'. I think a lot of him. And a saddle man afoot is a poor specimen."

"A saddle man thinking like an idiot is worse!" exploded the girl. "What sense was there in getting you out of town if you intend to go right back? So, you'll not go. You'll come right along to camp with me, where Aunt Lucy can fix up that wound of yours. I'd never forgive myself if I allowed you to go back now."

"But my bronc'?" argued Martell. "Old Inky will be missing me. I've got to get him."

"Your horse will be taken care of, too," the girl declared. "We're getting out of here!"

She let the fretting broncos go again and the rolling prairie swept to meet them, while all the time the long, jagged shadow of team and wagon raced out ahead of them, lengthening steadily as the sun dropped lower and lower behind them.

The sun lost itself in an exploding bomb of splendor beyond the far rim of the world and the anxiously waiting tide of shadow took over, laying banners of blue haze to cool the earth. North, the Lodestone Mountains laid a wide, darkening circle against the sky. In the incredibly far southern distances, seeming with little more substance than a line of cloud, the Selkirks lifted, lonely. And Bruce Martell, looking at it all and at the girl beside him, pondered the strangeness of one of the fullest days of his life.

Dusk had become dark when the spring wagon spun to a stop beside a settler wagon and a settler fire, from the radiance of which a gaunt figure stepped warily. The girl's call rang, clear and confident.

"Ezra, this is Tracy Carling. Would you do me a big favor?"

The gaunt figure came plodding out to the spring wagon. "Why, youngster," came a deep voice, "you know I will. What is it? Who's that ridin' with you? You were alone, goin' into town."

The settler stopped beside the wagon, peered

up at Martell and the girl. "Can't be your Uncle Brink. He's away, back to War Lance Creek. That hat . . . why this feller is a saddle man!"

"That's right," said Martell gravely. "The name is Bruce Martell."

He sensed the swift bristling of this gaunt settler, but the girl, speaking swiftly, began to explain. "So the only way I could get him to come along with me was to promise his horse would be taken care of. You told me this morning you were going into town tonight, Ezra. You could get Mister Martell's horse and bring it back with you."

"I could," admitted the settler, "though I ain't anxious to favor no saddle man, not with things goin' the way they are. Jason Spelle was by about sundown, givin' me the news. That Rockin' A crowd are gettin' rougher all the time with us settler folks." Ezra Banks shot a hard, abrupt question at Martell. "You ridin' for Asbell?"

"No. I'm on my own. Trying to locate my kid brother and the settler outfit he's with."

"A ridin' man's a ridin' man," grumbled Ezra Banks. "Still and all, long as Miss Tracy is askin' it of me . . . where's this horse of yours and what's it look like?"

"A black gelding," said Martell. "A big horse. Tied to the corral fence in back of the general store. Saddle cantle is stamped with three stars and there's a Winchester rifle slung to the rig."

"A'right," said Ezra Banks. "If the horse is still there, I'll bring it along. Girl, you better skedaddle. Your Aunt Lucy will be worryin' about you, though she's got company. Jason Spelle said he probably would be takin' the evenin' meal with you folks. And if you want my advice, young lady, you won't be pickin' up and totin' home every stray critter you run across. 'Specially ridin' men."

Ezra Banks turned and plodded back to his fire.

The wagon rolled on. Martell heard the girl's soft laughter. "Ezra is as crusty as an overdone loaf of bread," she said. "But his heart is pure gold and in the right place."

Within another half mile they topped still another roll of the prairie and dropped down into a wide swale that lay beyond. Here was another camp, its fire spiking the dark with ruddy cheer. The girl brought the spring wagon to a scudding stop.

"All safe and accounted for, Aunt Lucy!" she called cheerily. "Sorry I was late, but it couldn't be helped."

A man and woman stood beside the flames. The woman's hair had begun to whiten, but the remnants of what had been a vivid girlhood beauty still touched her with graciousness. Her eyes were very fine and now they softened with relief.

"Child," she answered, "I'd begun to worry. Who is that with you?"

Martell was abruptly uncomfortable. It had been growing on him in the past few minutes. Always a self-sufficient sort, to come trailing thus into a strange camp, just to get a skimpy knife wound tended, struck him as an embarrassing weakness. He wished now that he'd stuck to his first intention and gone back after his horse and taken care of his own troubles in his own way. But somehow, at the time, the girl's ideas had seemed to make sense.

He stepped down from the spring wagon and followed the girl over to the fire.

"This is Mister Martell, Aunt Lucy," the girl explained. "It's quite a story and I'll tell you all about it later. The main thing just now is a wound that must be tended. There was a ruckus in town and some stupid animal used a knife."

"Well, my goodness gracious sakes alive!" exclaimed Aunt Lucy. "You're nothing if not abrupt, child." But her fine eyes swung with quick sympathy, searching Martell's face. The firelight touched his left arm and hand and she saw the dark sogginess of his jumper and the still seeping scarlet on his hand. "Why," she cried, "you *are* wounded!"

"Ma'am," said Martell gravely, "I'm afraid there's a lot of fuss being made about little. It's only a scratch. I don't want to bother. . . ."

But Aunt Lucy, her first astonishment over, was already in action.

"You sit right by this fire, sir. Tracy girl, my medicine kit and my big scissors. Jason, push that water pot deeper into the fire. My gracious. Just a scratch, the man says. And here's his sleeve all soggy with blood."

Aunt Lucy helped Martell out of his jumper. With her scissors she cut away his soggy shirt sleeve and clucked to herself at sight of the ugly cut across his upper arm. She washed it carefully, smeared on some kind of healing ointment, and set a clean white bandage into place.

Martell crouched stoically by the fire, motionless while she worked. He was conscious of the fixed scrutiny of the man across the fire and lifted his eyes once to meet the fellow's glance. What he saw was not exactly enmity, but it was a hard and searching suspicion.

The girl had gone over to the big settler wagon that stood nearby, dark and gaunt against the first stars. Now she returned with a man's shirt, and Aunt Lucy nodded her approval. Finished with her bandage, she handed the shirt to Martell.

"One of my husband's," she said. "I had to ruin yours. Put this one on, then come back to the fire and we'll have some supper."

Martell rose to his feet. "Ma'am," he said, with a slow, quaint courtesy, "you have true gentleness in your heart."

He stepped off beyond the big wagon, donned the clean shirt. When he returned to the fire, there was a tin basin and warm water and a towel. He washed away the marks of his rough day and felt a new man.

Aunt Lucy, busy and deft, was setting out food and utensils on a square of tarpaulin spread by the fire. Yonder, just at the far edge of the firelight, the girl and the man stood, talking in low tones. It seemed to Martell that there was a faint touch of censure in the man's tone while the girl's brightness had become subdued.

Aunt Lucy announced supper and the girl and her companion moved up. The girl said: "Mister Martell, this is Jason Spelle."

Now, erect and more at ease, Martell was able to get a full measure of Jason Spelle. Spelle's height was equal to his own, with shoulders heavier but not as broad. And the man was thicker through the body, without Martell's lean suppleness of waist and hip. His hand grip told nothing, a brief touch, nothing more.

"Rocking A?" asked Spelle curtly.

"No," said Martell, matching Spelle's brusqueness of tone. "Just a man riding his own saddle into a new country."

This Jason Spelle had heavy, but handsome features, with a bold, arched nose that told of forcefulness, his age somewhere around Martell's own thirty years. He was dressed in a corduroy coat and trousers, flannel shirt with a dark, string tie. His boots were flat-heeled, a man of the soil, not the saddle. In the flicker of firelight his eyes looked brown, and told nothing.

Food was plain but ample, and Bruce Martell ate with honest hunger. He looked at the girl, but her eyes were on her plate. Even Aunt Lucy was silent, seeming to be waiting for an explanation of all this. Martell directed his quiet drawl at her.

"Just so you'll know you're not wasting kindness and hospitality on an out-and-out rascal, ma'am . . . here's how it happened." He went on, giving the story briefly. "I can see now," he ended, "where I didn't show the best of judgment in going off the edge like I did. Still and all, a man can take just so much pushing around."

Aunt Lucy's response warmed his heart. "In your place I'd have done the same," she declared. "Those three you speak of . . . who started the trouble . . . I wonder could they have been the Thorpes? Do you think it likely, Jason?"

Jason Spelle shrugged his heavy shoulders. "I'd have no way of knowing, Missus Carling. Only one thing I'm sure of. Our settler people can't be rightly blamed for their animosity toward saddle men . . . not after the kind of rough treatment Hack Asbell and his crowd have been throwing at them. You haven't heard of the latest piece of deviltry Asbell has cooked up. His men have been barging into some of the settler camps, bullying the folks around, and going through their wagons. That sort of high-handed business isn't making our people love saddle men more."

"Going through the wagons? You mean, robbing them?"

"Well, not exactly robbing, perhaps," conceded Spelle. "Though that could be the next step. The excuse they have cooked up is the claim that settlers are slow-elking Rocking A beef and that, in going through settler wagons, they're searching for some of that meat. There's no truth to it, of course . . . the slow-elking talk, I mean. It's just another of Hack Asbell's lies. The man is full of them."

Bruce Martell had no wish to start an argument in this camp. But there was a dominant assertiveness of certainty in Jason Spelle's manner and words that stirred a vague irritation in him. He said: "You could be wrong, Spelle, about the slow-elking angle. For there is some of it going on."

"How would you know?"

"I saw the evidence of it. This morning, on my way in across the Lodestone foothills. Four Rocking A critters. Definitely slow-elked."

"What makes you so sure?" There was a thread of sharpness in Spelle's words.

Martell's irritation with the man grew. He didn't like the tone; he didn't like the manner. It came to him abruptly that he plain didn't like Jason Spelle, didn't like any part of him at all. But he managed to keep any hint of his feeling out of his own voice.

"A slow-elker," he drawled, "always leaves his trademark. He butchers wastefully. In this case only the choice parts of the carcasses had been taken, the loins and haunches. The rest was left to the coyotes and buzzards."

Aunt Lucy spoke impulsively. "What a shame. I can't abide wastefulness. You can't blame Hack Asbell for being angry over that sort of thing, Jason."

"Perhaps not . . . if it was slow-elking. But Asbell could have done the butchering himself, just as an excuse to carry on some of his high-handed business, like this searching of settler camps and bullying people around."

"That," said Martell bluntly, "doesn't even make good sense, Spelle. If Asbell felt that way, he could have just made talk that way, without wasting four critters back in a lonely little creek meadow, where nobody would see the actual evidence, nobody but the coyotes and buzzards. It was just chance that I stumbled on that meadow myself."

"You talk as though Asbell was a friend of yours," charged Spelle.

"Not a friend . . . not an enemy," retorted Martell. "I met the man for the first time in my life this morning at the scene of the slow-elking. He was pretty worked up, and he had a right to be. In his boots I'd have come to a boil myself."

It was the girl, Tracy, who saw how this thing was heading and spoke now to head it off. Even so, she was on Jason Spelle's side.

"What you saw with your own eyes, you saw, Mister Martell. But that doesn't excuse the Rocking A for going through settler camps and wagons as though everybody in Indio Basin were guilty."

"No, it doesn't." Martell nodded. Then he added, with gentle censure: "No more than it entitles settlers to curse and threaten me, just because I'm a saddle man. I've found there's nearly always two sides to every question." He turned to Aunt Lucy. "For all your kindness, ma'am . . . if there's any chores needing doing, I'll be happy to oblige."

The older woman met his glance, gravely intent. Now she smiled. "There is strong independence in you, isn't there? I know you'll feel better, so, if you'll be careful of that arm, you can unharness the spring wagon team and care for them and the other horses. There's a pool at the head of the swale where you can water them."

Martell built a cigarette and went willingly about these chores. He wanted to get away from that fire while Jason Spelle was there. The man's personality dragged roughly across his own and further contact would be sure to strike sparks. And Martell wanted to be no cause of even the slightest unpleasantness about this camp that had shown him so much kindness and hospitality.

Aside from a slight ache and some growing stiffness, his arm did not bother him and the increasing brilliance of the starlight aided him in his chores.

Off to one side of the camp stood still another team of broncos, harnessed to a buckboard, which Martell assumed belonged to Jason Spelle. As he came back from the spring pool, leading a pair of big, staunch heavy-wagon horses, he saw Spelle and the girl move out toward the buckboard. They stood there for some time, their figures blending with the shadow bulk of the buckboard. And then, as Martell, finished with what he was doing, came back to the fire, the buckboard whirled away into the night. Presently the girl slipped back to the fire.

Supper things had been washed and put away. Aunt Lucy, of the type who found happiness in eternal busyness, had a bit of sewing in her lap at which she worked in the firelight. She nipped off a bit of thread with her teeth, looked at Martell.

"My husband should be back tomorrow. He went out to War Lance Creek again after some gear he left there, plows and such. He wants to fallow our land before the first rains come. I imagine you've had little experience with a plow, Mister Martell?"

Martell met her brief smile with one of his own. "None at all, ma'am. That kind of rigging just isn't my line. Cattle are what I savvy best.

44

And humans." He glanced around. "Pretty lonely camp for just a couple of women."

Aunt Lucy laughed. "Daytimes there's nothing to worry about. And at night Tracy and I fort up in the big wagon. We can both shoot a gun. And Jason Spelle drops by regularly to see that we're all right. Then there's Ezra Banks, our nearest neighbor. Ezra says for us just to yell, day or night, and, as he puts it, he'd come a-runnin'." She laughed again merrily.

Martell's slow smile broke up the dark gravity of his face. "Have to be quite a yell, ma'am . . . to reach to Ezra."

Martell built another cigarette and the pale smoke curled up about his lean head and lost itself in the night. Now the darkness brought a new sound, the mutter of running hoofs, coming in from the north. The girl, Tracy Carling, sitting, cross-legged, beside her aunt, staring at the fire flames, lifted her head and listened.

"The Rocking A," she said. "I sometimes wish, Aunt Lucy, that Uncle Brink hadn't settled so close to the trail that the Rocking A uses, going and coming from town."

"Nonsense," chided Aunt Lucy cheerfully. "I'm quite sure Hack Asbell and his crew never intend us any harm. I'll have to speak to Jason Spelle and tell him not to fill your head so full of fears of Hack Asbell. I sometimes grow a little impatient with Jason on that score. Why he should insist that Asbell is such an ogre, I don't know. Certainly we've never been bothered."

"Looks like you might be tonight, ma'am," said Bruce Martell, getting to his feet. "Unless that trail heads right next to this camp, those hoofs are leading right in here."

This was true. There could be no mistake. That massed beat of running horses was heading straight into this camp across the swale.

"You see," declared the girl. "Jason was right."

"They wouldn't dare!" said Aunt Lucy spiritedly. "I'll give them a piece of my mind. . . ."

"Ma'am," said Martell, "I think it would be smart for you womenfolk to get back by the big wagon, out of the firelight. It's a good place to argue from . . . the dark. If you please, ma'am."

He had Aunt Lucy by the arm, helping her to her feet, and he almost unceremoniously herded her and the girl back into the shadows. He used the shadows himself, then waited, alert and still.

The pound of hoofs massed to a sudden roll, and then there were a full half dozen riders swinging about the outer rim of the firelight, pulling to a milling halt, restless hoofs chopping up a fine haze of dust. There was one in advance of the rest, and Martell recognized him instantly. It was Carp Bastion, the burly, intolerant foreman of the Rocking A. His eyes were stabbing the dark beyond the fire with a hot impatience and his voice rolled, rough and arrogant.

"Come out of that dark, sod-buster. I want a look at you. And I want a look through that wagon, too. How much slow-elking Rocking A beef have you got stashed around here? You heard me! Come out into the firelight, or I come over there after you. Hurry up!"

Behind him, Bruce Martell heard Tracy Carling catch her breath in sharp indignation, heard a stir of movement as though either she or her aunt intended to answer Bastion's order and move into the light. With a slow sweep of his left arm, Martell motioned them back. And so he waited, saying nothing, but poised and alert for anything.

He's not just sure, thought Martell. *He doesn't know how many, or who, whether men or women. And he doesn't know whether there's a gun looking at him. But he's too bull-headed, too intolerant to wait and find out. He'll be coming to see.*

This was what Martell wanted, what he was waiting for. At all odds, gunfire couldn't be risked, not with the two women there and in the open. Besides, the set-up was wrong. Out there the odds were too heavy. But if Bastion would come over—apart from the rest. . . .

Martell drew his gun, switched it to his left hand. And that was when Carp Bastion, full of that blistering, headlong arrogance, came over, cursing as he sent his horse plunging across the circle of firelight and into the thin dark beside the wagon.

Chapter Four

Swift shift from the dark into the light, then into the dark again, could play tricks with a man's eyesight. So Bruce Martell had the advantage of being a half-guessed shadow to Carp Bastion in the brief second it took for Martell to glide in beside Bastion's horse. And Martell's right hand, clawing out, settled solid and sure on Bastion's belt.

Martell put his back into the pull, and had Bastion toppling before the cowboy could set himself to resist. Bastion's wild grab at his saddle horn missed, and the blur of surprised curses ended abruptly as he hit the ground.

Martell dropped on him, sinking a knee into the small of Bastion's back and at the same time he drove the muzzle of his gun boring against the side of Bastion's head. Then Martell let his voice go, harsh and dominant, across the night.

"Everybody out there stay put! I've got a gun against this fellow's head, and if you want him back alive . . . watch yourselves!"

After that, Martell held his breath, wondering if it was going to work. Sweat broke across his face. Those two women in back of him—if they were only somewhere else and out of line!

The riders beyond the fire broke up the mass of

their group, spinning their horses back into the full dark like a covey of startled quail, and the high hard cry of one of them rang thin and wicked.

"Carp! Give us the word, Carp!"

"Give it to them," gritted Martell, boring the muzzle of his gun savagely against Bastion's head. "Quick! Give it. Or you can die right here!"

Carp Bastion was raging, but that cold gun muzzle was a bitter persuader. Besides, the shock of complete surprise had broken through his arrogance, at least for the moment.

"Wait it out . . . wait it out!" he yelled thickly. "Don't start anything!"

A few taut and deadly seconds ticked away. Then: "Carp . . . where are you? What the devil's goin' on there? Carp . . . ?"

"Carp's down on the ground," answered Martell. "He's not hurt yet. But he will be, if anything breaks. I mean it. If you want him alive, take it slow."

Out in the dark, riders swore and milled helplessly, not knowing exactly what to do. But those very dangerous first moments had passed, and Bruce Martell drew a slow, deep breath of relief.

"Listen close, Carp," he murmured. "Like this morning, you still talk too much. But what you say now had better make sense and get results. Tell your men to be on their way to wherever they were going. Tell them if they do that, you'll be along to join them later, no worse for wear than you are now. It's your neck, Carp. I mean business. All right . . . tell 'em."

Carp did. No man could long occupy the position of being facedown on the earth with a heavy knee in the small of his back and the muzzle of a gun against his head without realizing that for this moment, at least, he had no luck at all. So Carp, his face down, yelled muffled orders.

"Clear out! Get goin'! I'll meet you in town. Don't argue. Move out!"

"But Carp . . . !"

"Damn it!" bawled Carp. "Do as you're told. You heard me. Move out!"

There were bewildered growls and some frustrated cursing. Then the roll of hoofs moved off into the night and faded out with distance. Martell lifted Bastion's gun, straightened up, and stepped back.

"All right," he rapped. "You can get up now. But mind your manners and lay off that cussing. There are ladies around."

Bastion got to his feet and at gun muzzle Martell urged him out into the firelight, where the Rocking A foreman twisted his head and got his first look at Martell. His eyes congested with rage.

"You!" he exploded thickly. "You . . . again! The second time you've mauled me out of my saddle. You . . . !"

"Careful, Carp. Mind your language. Yeah, me

again. Monotonous, I know. But you will barge into things. I don't enjoy the chore of hauling you around like a sack of wheat myself. But it seems you just won't learn. Now cool off and talk sense. Just what was your real business in barging into this camp, full of bullyrag and noise?"

"You heard me say why when I first rode in!" exploded the raging but helpless cowboy. "I'm lookin' for slow-elked Rockin' A beef. With your own eyes you saw four Rockin' A beef that had been slow-elked. Well, I'm lookin' for that meat and I intend to find it, if I have to search every sod-buster wagon from here to the Selkirks. Now you know!"

"Asbell's orders?" prodded Martell.

Carp Bastion's hesitation was slight but unmistakable. "That's neither here or there, and in some things a man don't need any orders. I'm Rockin' A. The other boys are Rockin' A. We look after Rockin' A affairs."

"You're doing a poor job of it," Martell declared bluntly. "You're hurting more than helping with this sort of business. Use you head, man. You can't bully five hundred settlers. But you can lose your neck trying."

"When I need advice from you, I'll let you know," said Bastion sullenly. "And here's something you better understand, right here and now. From now on you're open game as far as Rockin' A is concerned. And you and me . . . just

51

the two of us . . . well, that's a chunk of future business apart from all the other business. Maybe you're good, maybe you're just lucky. One of these days I expect to find out."

"We won't worry about that just now," Martell drawled calmly. "Right now, though, here's some advice you better take, whether you like it or not. This particular settler camp is definitely off bounds for Rocking A. Very fine folks, these. Friends of mine. You come bothering them again and that piece of business between you and me that you just spoke of will explode and rain down all over you. Look me in the eye, man."

These last words had a snap to them. Carp looked, and what he saw made him blink and shift uncomfortably. He mumbled: "How long you keepin' me here?"

"Not long. Miss Carling, would you bring the gentleman's horse over here, please?"

Bastion's horse, after losing its rider so unceremoniously, had swung and backed nervously away, reins trailing. But the girl had no trouble now in catching it and leading it over to the fire. A glance told Martell all he wanted. There was no saddle weapon of any sort. He jerked the shells from Bastion's belt gun and handed it to the burly, but now subdued, cowboy.

"All right, Carp," he said. "You can pull out."

Bastion went into his saddle, then looked down at Martell. "What the devil kind of man are you?"

he burst out. "The marks of a lifelong saddle man are on you, yet here you are hanging out in a sod-buster camp, and standin' up for them."

"It could be the people, Carp," drawled Martell. "You ought to know them better. Broaden you, maybe."

Bastion swung his head, as though unable to understand. There was nothing flexible in Bastion's reasoning. His code was simple enough. The cattleman was king. His world was a cattleman's world. There was little place in it for anything else, and definitely no place for a sod-buster. His hate for the man with a plow was as ancient as the cattle business itself. He would have spurred away then, but Aunt Lucy appeared suddenly beside Martell.

"Have I ever harmed you?" she asked Carp Bastion quietly.

He looked at her, at the soft order of her whitening hair, at the grave, kindly simplicity in her eyes and face. And he swung restlessly in his saddle.

"No, ma'am," he blurted awkwardly, "reckon you never did. Yet. . . ."

"Yet I'm a sod-buster, as you call us settlers," cut in Aunt Lucy. "I'm no different than the rest."

Carp Bastion was out of his depth. He didn't know what to say. Under the calm serenity of this aging woman's glance he felt cornered and at a loss for words to get out of this thing gracefully.

53

"You have my word for one thing," said Aunt Lucy. "There is no stolen Rocking A beef in this camp, and there never will be. My niece, my husband, and myself . . . we are respectable people. We have no quarrel with anyone, least of all with Mister Asbell and the Rocking A. You believe me, don't you?"

"Yes'm," mumbled Carp Bastion. "Yes'm. I reckon I do." In desperation he set spurs to his horse and tore away through the night.

Martell reached for his smoking. "I think," he said quietly, "that Carp will be a better man after tonight. You've started him thinking, ma'am."

"I . . . I hope so," said Aunt Lucy. She dropped a hand on Martell's arm, let out a little shak sigh. "I was frightened half to death, for a moment there."

"So was I," agreed Martell. "I kept thinking of you womenfolk. It wasn't very pretty, the way I played it. But there didn't seem any other way. Carp, in his saddle, with his men behind him . . . that was one thing that talk or argument wouldn't have done a thing against. And even if I'd thrown a gun, then it wouldn't have done any good. They'd have taken a chance with their numbers. So I had to get Carp away from the rest and then work fast. But it worked out all right." He looked down at Aunt Lucy with his slow, warming smile.

"It was our good fortune that Tracy brought you

into camp," she said simply. "Thank you, Bruce Martell."

The girl was standing by the fire, looking at Martell, yet not looking at him. That was the way Martell felt. It was something he couldn't put into words, the way she was looking at him without putting her eyes directly on him.

"Violence seems to come your way no matter where you ride or where you stop, doesn't it?" she said.

Martell's smile lingered. "It's been what you might call a full day," he admitted dryly.

"You and that man . . . you'd met before?"

"This morning." Martell nodded. "Back at the scene of the slow-elking."

"And you had trouble with him then?"

This Tracy Carling, thought Martell, was keen as a knife blade. She hadn't missed a word of what had passed between him and Carp. "We argued a mite," he admitted.

"And so there must be a third meeting," she said gravely. "He promised that, didn't he? And that will be . . . what?"

The gravity of Martell's face came back. "Probably nothing at all. I think we're beginning to understand each other, Carp and me. He's not a bad sort. Knowing him better I might like him. And tomorrow is another day. I never bother trouble."

They settled down about the fire again. Now the

stars were out in their full tide, whitening the sky above, shining a deceptive silver sheen over the wide and resting world beneath. A little breeze stirred, rustling close to the earth, frightening the fire flames until they bent and dodged and wove, then running on to other mild deviltry. It carried a freshness with it, and the smell of space.

Again the night brought the sound of hoofs, slowly moving this time, and bringing no trouble. It was Ezra Banks, riding Martell's big black gelding. The gaunt settler swung down.

"Your horse, like I promised," he said to Martell in his deep, slow way. "And a good 'un. Even-minded and soft ridin'. Too good a bronc' to be left stranded in town because you went and got yourself mixed up in a row with them no-good Thorpe brothers."

"I knew it!" exclaimed Aunt Lucy. "I knew it would be the Thorpes who started the trouble with Mister Martell. You heard about it in town, Ezra?"

"I reckon, Lucy Carling. But from all accounts, right about now them Thorpes are wishin' they hadn't. Bully Thorpe, he's nursin' a face half-caved in from a beer bottle. And Dyke Thorpe, he ain't in much better shape, but swearin' he won't miss with his knife, next time. And Whip Thorpe, well, he ain't as bad messed up as the others, but he's got marks that won't wear off for a day or two. I'd say that for a couple of weeks at least the world will be free of their cussedness."

Bruce Martell had stepped past Ezra Banks while the gaunt settler was talking, eager to touch and speak to his horse again. The black greeted him with a little nicker, rubbed its head against his shoulder. Martell petted the animal a moment, then turned to Ezra Banks.

"If you'll accept them from a saddle man, old-timer . . . I'm offering you my thanks."

Ezra Banks cleared his throat. "*Humph!* You're welcome. But I'd 'a' felt kinda put on about, if you hadn't handled them Thorpes as well as you did. Yeah, you're welcome."

The fire had begun to shrink toward coals. Ezra Banks dropped on his gaunt heels beside it, spread gnarled hands across the warmth, for a slight chill had begun to let down across the night. He twisted his head toward Martell.

"When you and Miss Tracy come by this evenin', you said you were tryin' to locate a brother in this basin, Martell. You got any idee at all where to look?"

"None at all," Martell told him. "If I had, I wouldn't have been prowling here and yon, bumping into trouble."

Ezra Banks stared at the ruby coals. "Never heard the name Martell before, so I reckon I can't help you there."

"He's with a man named Clebourne . . . Jeff Clebourne."

Ezra's head jerked up. "Jeff Clebourne? Well,

now . . . that's different. I know Jeff Clebourne. Met him back on War Lance Creek before the jump-off. Had a young feller with him, drivin' his second wagon. Jest a sprig, curly-headed. Allus on the go, this young feller was, restless as a colt in spring sunshine. Seems I remember Jeff callin' him Kit or . . ."

"Kip?" put in Martell.

"That's it. Kip. That your brother?"

"Right. You know where Clebourne set his stakes, old-timer?"

"Not exactly, but I got a general idee. Jeff Clebourne, he'd had a look at this basin. When the word first got out that the government was considerin' openin' Indio Basin for settlement, Jeff made a trip in here to sorta prospect the land. Back on War Lance Creek he told me he kinda liked the looks of a piece somewhere along the south bank of the Hayfork River, along the west reach of it. So I calculate that's where Jeff headed. You hit the river and foller it west and you might have luck."

"My luck was in meeting up with people like you and the Carlings, Ezra."

The gaunt settler got to his feet, prepared to head back to his own camp. "Should you meet up with Hack Asbell, see can you persuade the ornery old buzzard that at least some of us is fair-to-middlin' decent folks. Mebbe he'll leave us alone, then. 'Night, Lucy . . . Tracy, girl. Iffen

58

Brink needs help to unload when he gits in, tell him to holler. See you again, Martell."

Ezra Banks plodded off into the dark.

Martell turned to the womenfolk. "For everything, thanks again," he said gravely. "Maybe the time will come when I'll have a chance to return some of your kindness."

"Oh!" exclaimed Aunt Lucy, "but you're not going to ride any farther tonight, are you? Put the idea right out of your mind, sir. You camp right here by this fire. Tracy and I will both sleep better for knowing there's a man around. You go tend to your horse and we'll get some blankets from the wagon for you. Tomorrow is plenty of time to go on after your brother."

So that was the way it was. Martell unsaddled, watered the black, and turned the horse loose to forage, knowing it would not stir far from the other horses munching beyond the wagons. When he got back to the fire, a pad of blankets awaited him.

The womenfolk had retired to beds in the big wagon. Martell could hear them murmuring back and forth as he smoked a final cigarette, watching the last dwindling glow of the fire, the fading coals winking redly through a powdering of gray ash.

In the sky the stars spilled their eternal chilling glitter, watching the vast roll and turn of the earth still into sleep. The tensions of the long day ran out of Martell, letting weariness move in. He took a final drag at his cigarette, tossed the butt into the fire ash, rolled up in the blankets. Some time later he awakened to hear the roll of hoofs beating by in the dark, heading north. The Rocking A, riding home, no doubt. The cadence of speeding horses faded and died in the distance. Martell went back to sleep.

Chapter Five

The sun was an hour high the next morning when Bruce Martell struck the south bank of Hayfork River and turned west along it. Behind him, at the Carling camp, he had left two women who had made a stronger impression upon him than any of their sex since the days of his own mother. And from Aunt Lucy, at least, he'd had a warm invitation to visit them again.

The girl, Tracy, had been gracious and not unfriendly, but had shown a reserve that was slightly puzzling. She had been, Martell mused, easier to talk to on the ride out from town the previous afternoon after snagging him away from that mob of crazy settlers. Her reserve, her vague impression of withdrawing, came after they had reached the Carling camp, after his incipient argument with Jason Spelle.

Well, that could be the answer. Maybe there was something between her and Jason Spelle, and Spelle had chided her for taking the part of a strange saddle man. Either way, it was a part of something that had passed, another day marked off with all the other yesterdays.

On his way up to the river, Martell passed several settler camps. He swung wide of these. Even so, twice he saw men watching him warily from the distance and the early morning sunlight glinted on weapons they held. These were harsh reminders that the rough doings of yesterday had not been due to casual circumstances. Hate and enmity had not died with the night. It was here again to greet this fair new morning. It was something that lay across this land like some pale and shifting menace. And Martell, old in experience with such things, knew that it was a menace that would only be wiped away by the searing flame of guns.

It would, he told himself, come certainly to that, men being what they were. Few of them reasoned with their heads, many of them with their passions, which were blind and brutal things. Men always learned the hard way. They had to be hurt savagely before they put reason ahead of force.

In itself, this Hayfork River was a pleasant stream. Big, gaunt oak trees spread wide blots of pleasant shade along its higher banks, while lines of willow and alder hugged the main watercourse between the spreading gravel flats built up by past freshets. As always, the bounty of water and cover attracted wildlife. Coveys of quail buzzed and called about the willow thickets and in the green façades of wild grapevines climbing high among the alders. Smaller bird life was everywhere and across deep, cool pools, wood ducks splashed and glided.

At midmorning Martell crossed a small creek coming into the river at right angles, and he paused here to let the black horse drink. Beyond stretched a wide, deep-earthed flat, lush and thick with sun-dried grass. Moving on up to the level of this, Martell saw, some four hundred yards ahead, two wagons drawn up in the shade of a big oak. A little apart from the wagons a man stood, a rifle across his arm. Drawn up in front of him in a thin semicircle were three riders. There was grim portent in the picture.

Martell's first thought was to swing wide and ride around this thing. But this was the first camp he'd run across in quite a distance, and here-abouts somewhere, according to what Ezra Banks had told him, he might find the Clebourne camp. This could be the very camp he was looking for, and if he rode around it, then what? Maybe the figure with the rifle was Kip, his kid brother.

No, that wasn't Kip. The kid was of a more slender build, not as tall. Just the same, something nagged at the back of Martell's mind, intuition, prescience—something pushing him forward. Hard-headed, practical, he fought against it. He'd had trouble enough yesterday. This could be none of his mix. Yet, he shook the reins and the black lifted to a fast jog, taking him straight in toward the wagons. He had cut the distance to less than a third before the three riders became aware of his approach; the man with the rifle must have seen him from the moment he lifted out of that little watercourse back there.

The riders broke up their semicircle, swung, then bunched, warily watching both him and the settler. Martell was high and alert in the saddle as he cut down the distance. And then, presently, there he was, within fifty feet of them, letting the hard pressure of his scrutiny run across them.

There was a thread of desperation in the settler's voice as he boomed, "You, too, can stop right there!"

"You've nothing to fear from me, friend," answered Martell. "These others . . . what about them?"

There was uncertainty in the settler's reply. "I don't know. They're not Rocking A. They're looking for somebody. They say he's around this camp. I say he ain't. They don't believe me."

"No, by God!" growled one of the riders, "we don't. You admit your name is Clebourne. The word I picked along the way is that Kip Martell came into this basin with you, driving your second wagon. Where is he?"

Bruce Martell had his good look at the speaker. Inside, he was chill and taut. Outwardly the only sign of this was in the darkening of his eyes, that look brushed with smoke.

This fellow he was looking at, what would he

be wanting with Kip? And this was the Clebourne camp—but where was Kip? Martell edged the black closer.

The settler swung his rifle in a little arc. "Move along, the lot of you," he said tautly. "This is my camp. Stay out of it!"

Martell did not watch the settler any more, but he missed no move, no shade of expression of the other three.

"You heard what the man said," he drawled coldly. "I'm sure he means you. Move on!"

The leader of the three was swarthy, with a broad, blocky face and black, round eyes. There was a snaky fixedness about them, just as hard, just as cruel.

"You'd be siding this sod-buster?" he growled.

"Could be. Yes, I think so. Changes the picture, doesn't it?"

"Maybe . . . maybe not!"

"It does. Move on!"

The swarthy one shifted a little in his saddle. His black eyes flickered. Uncertainty was beginning to work in him.

"You could be good," he blurted, "or you could be ordinary. The issue ain't big enough to find out . . . now."

He spun his horse and spurred away, the other two pounding after him. The settler lowered his rifle and spoke with some bewilderment. "Well, I will be damned. Never expected to see the day when a saddle man would take my part against others like him. What do you want?"

Martell answered him with a question. "That fellow was right . . . your name is Clebourne?"

The settler nodded. He was a big man, bearded. "Yeah. I'm Jeff Clebourne."

"If Kip Martell isn't here, where is he? I'm Kip's brother Bruce."

"I'll be twice damned!" exclaimed Clebourne. "Get down, man. You're plenty welcome. Kip's been wondering when you'd show. Yeah, Kip's right here. But I couldn't tell Horgan that, could I?"

"Horgan?" Martell swung his head, stared after the vanishing three. "That fellow was Pitch Horgan?"

"None other. First time I ever saw him in my life, but from Kip's description, I couldn't be mistaken. Yeah, that was Horgan."

As Martell stepped from the saddle, Clebourne turned toward the river and waved a long arm. Two figures came scrambling immediately into view, and hurried toward the wagons. One of them carried a rifle, and Martell knew this one at a glance. Along with Clebourne he moved to meet them.

Recognition came from the other side. "Bruce!" came the yell. "Bruce! The old lone wolf himself!"

Martell's eyes softened. He gripped the kid's

hand, wrapped his other arm around him. He thought he saw the kid blink rapidly a couple of times.

"This is him, folks," chortled Kip. "Look him over. Didn't I tell you that when this big, tough nut came riding in, then the coyotes'd get off the trail? Well, you just saw what I meant."

He pulled Bruce around. "These are my people, Bruce. Jeff and Cadence Clebourne." He said it again. "My people."

That slim figure that had come running up from the river with Kip, she stood, lithe and brown and big-eyed, in her denim shirt and faded jeans. Maybe nineteen or twenty years old, Bruce guessed, with a shadow of some fear, still far back in her eyes. Bruce gave her that faint, slow-breaking smile.

"Kip's people are my people," he said. "I'm happy to know you both." He shook hands with Jeff Clebourne. He turned back to Kip. "What's Pitch Horgan doing here, kid?"

The exuberance died out of Kip's face. "Tell you about it later. I didn't enjoy skulking back there behind the riverbank. But don't think Jeff was facing them alone." He shook his rifle. "I had a bead on Horgan every second. If he'd made one phony move, I'd have cut him in half. But Jeff thought if he could put over the bluff of me not being here anymore, it would be the best way out. There was . . . Cadence to think of."

67

Kip looked at the girl, and in that glance Bruce read a lot. He didn't press the point, slapping Kip on the shoulder again. "Good to find you, kid. I started out, soon as I got your letter. Quite a country, this. Something I never expected, though. That you'd become a man of the soil."

Kip grinned. "Sod-buster, you mean. Well, things happen, and a man's ideas change. Get the kak off that horse of yours and make yourself at home. This is home now, Bruce, and you're not going anywhere."

While Bruce took care of the black, the Clebournes, father and daughter, showing a fine consideration, busied themselves about camp chores, leaving Bruce and Kip together.

"All right, kid," said Bruce quietly. "How about Horgan? You're not running away from anything, are you?"

"Only from a life that came near making a damned fool of me," answered Kip simply. "Or maybe it's better this way . . . from being a bigger jack than I had been. Sure, I was getting pretty wild, riding with Pitch and his crowd. I ain't claiming any credit for breaking away from them in time. Put it that I was just lucky. Anyhow, I was flat on my back in a boarding house at Brenner Station, getting over a case of plain, old-fashioned measles when Horgan and the gang made the big break and pulled a rustling job, back in the Madeline Plains country. That's where the luck came in. If I hadn't been sick, I'd probably have been in on that job with them. Bruce, I was a lot of fool there for a while, wasn't I?"

"There were times when I was pretty worried, all right," admitted Bruce. "For I'd heard some talk down the country about a guy named Horgan who had all the earmarks of getting outside the law, sooner or later. And there were reports that you'd been seen with him. I was all set to ride in and drag you off by the scruff of the neck as soon as that marshal job I'd contracted for in Rawhide was finished. There was a sizable bonus guaranteed me if I'd stick the full year, and I wanted that bonus. So I kept my fingers crossed and stuck it out. But . . . go on."

"Well," said Kip, "I stuck around Brenner Station for a time, getting my strength back, doing odd jobs for my keep. A couple of settler wagons came through, heading for War Lance Creek, where the jump-off of a land rush into Indio Basin was to start. Driving one of those wagons was a girl. She looked at me and I looked at her. Right then I knew I was all done with Pitch Horgan. I got to know that girl and her father."

"The Clebournes?" asked Bruce.

"Right. Jeff asked me if I'd be interested in coming along to Indio Basin. He said that while Cadence could drive a wagon as good as any man in ordinary traveling, it was sure to be a wild, rough stampede when the jump-off scramble really started and he didn't want Cadence trying to fight a wagon through it alone. The proposition suited me, right down to the ground. So I wrote you the letter then, telling you where you could find me, where I was going."

"But why would Horgan be looking for you, kid?"

"I'm coming to that," said Kip soberly. "There was a 'breed, Lip Matole. He showed up and braced me the night before we pulled out of Brenner Station. Matole was one of Horgan's crowd and he said Horgan had sent him after me. That rustling deal on the Madeline Plains had cost Horgan a couple of men and he was short-handed for another job he was figuring on. I told Matole nothing doing, that I was cutting loose from the old crowd and going my own way. Matole began getting mean about it. He'd seen me with the Clebournes and pretty soon he made a crack about Cadence. That seemed to blow something loose in my head. Next thing I knew I was looking at Matole through smoke . . . and he was down."

Kip scrubbed a nervous hand through his curly hair. "I thought that would finish me with Jeff and Cadence, sure. I told them the whole story, all of it, right from the first. I didn't leave out a thing. I didn't make any excuses. When I got through, they hadn't changed a bit. They still wanted me to come along. Bruce, they're the finest people in the world."

Bruce nodded with satisfaction. "I'm happy about the whole thing, kid. To know you've rubbed out the old trail and are now on a new and good one. Don't let the memory of that Matole *hombre* bother you."

"I won't, if Horgan'll let it be that way. But Matole was a favorite of Horgan's and it looks like Horgan is out to find me and even up for him. I had no idea Horgan was here in Indio Basin, until a few days ago. A friend of Jeff's dropped by and said he'd met up with a guy who was asking around, trying to locate me. He described Horgan, so I knew the shadow of the old days was still hanging over me. Since then I've been like a flea on a hot griddle, dodging for that riverbank every time a man in a saddle shows up. I don't like that sort of stuff. If I were on my own, I'd hunt Horgan up and tell him to cut his wolf loose. I'm not afraid of him. But I've got to consider Cadence. I don't want her to ever have to look at me and remember any other dead man besides Lip Matole. Damn Horgan, anyhow! Why can't he leave me alone?"

"We'll see if that can't be taken care of, kid," said Bruce. "You've got the right idea. Keep out of his way, and let nature take its course."

Chapter Six

The Rocking A headquarters stood at the head of a long, sloping flat in the Lodestone foothills some three miles north of the Hayfork River. A bachelor outfit, everything about it was built entirely for utility. There were no frills. What Hack Asbell was pleased to call his ranch house was a three-roomed cabin, no more, with a narrow porch running across the short front of it.

Hack Asbell stood on this porch and stared down across the morning sunshine at the rider coming up the flat on a big black gelding. Asbell turned his grizzled head and yelled.

"Carp!"

Carp Bastion stepped out of the bunkhouse opposite.

Asbell said: "Take a look."

Carp did and swore, first in surprise, then with growling satisfaction. "I don't know what would be bringin' him here, Hack, but whatever it is and when it's done with, I want a private word with that jigger. Just him and me. Twice he got the jump on me. This time we'll start from the same line."

"You want to die young, Carp?" scoffed Asbell. "You're ordinary as hell with a gun. But that *hombre*, he's got the earmarks all over him."

"I ain't talkin' about guns," said Carp. "I ain't got that much against him. I'm goin' to have one of the boys get the drop on him and make him take his gun off. Then him and me'll toe the scratch and I'll find out, one way or the other."

Asbell's smile was thinly dry. "You're a funny one, Carp. Just like a damned kid at times. You just got to know whether you can lick a guy or whether you can't. It could be interesting. But if he knocks your ears back, remember you went hunting for it."

"He knocks 'em back, I won't cry." Carp dodged back into the bunkhouse.

Asbell was smoking a black cheroot. He rolled it from one grim lip to the other as he watched Bruce Martell ride up. Martell came in steadily, loose and easy in his saddle, eyes lazy but alert. He pulled in and inclined his head.

"Howdy! Glad to find you home, Mister Asbell. Got time for a little talk?"

"Thought I told you to stay the other side of the river," growled Asbell.

"True," murmured Bruce. "But here I am. Your fur was considerable rumpled then. I'm gambling it's smoothed down some since."

"I still say I'll hang the first damned slow-elker I come across," snapped Asbell acidly. "But . . . light and have your say."

Bruce stepped from the saddle, moved up on the cabin porch, and reached for his smoking. He

73

was silent while he built his cigarette. Asbell stirred restlessly.

"What's on your mind?"

"Beef," said Bruce. "Beef to feed hungry settlers."

Asbell swung around. "Friend," he said, with thin harshness, "that's a touchy subject with me. You ought to know that."

Martell nodded. "I know. But this is a legitimate deal, with profit for you and for me. I want to buy some beef stock from you."

"How many and what for?"

"About a dozen head to start with. And . . ."

"And you'd slaughter 'em and peddle the meat to those damned sod-busters, eh?" cut in Asbell.

"The general idea. There are some other details."

"No!" rapped Asbell. "Not a chance. Not a pound of Rocking A beef ever goes to feed them cussed sod-busters."

"But they are eating some of it, by your own admission," Martell pointed out. "I saw one job of slow-elking against you. You said there'd been more of the same. You're not making any money out of your cattle that way. You raise cows to sell, don't you?"

"Not to sod-busters," Asbell vowed. "I'll drive my beef across the Lodestones through Fandango Pass and on down to the railroad at Quartz Junction, same as in the past. That kind of business is good enough for me. To hell with the sod-busters. Let 'em starve, for all I care. As for the slow-elking . . . I'll bust that up, if I have to hire me an outfit of fifty men."

Bruce Martell stood silent for a moment. "That sun out there," he said musingly, "it rises and it sets. The earth turns. Things change and nothing stands still. The world moves along and a man moves with it, or it rolls him under and crushes him. You know those settlers are in Indio Basin to stay, Mister Asbell. Why beat your head to pieces against the inevitable?"

Asbell clamped dogged teeth into his cheroot. "Sure I know they're there to stay. I knew the day would come when they'd overrun Indio Basin. That's why I got my roots set here on this side of the river. They stay south of the river and leave my beef alone and I won't bother 'em. Hell, I'm no fool. I know what a man can do and what he can't. Pushing them sod-busters out of the basin is one of the things I can't do. But that's no sign I got to like 'em, is it? Or sell beef to 'em? No, by God. I did all right the old way and I'll stay by the old way."

"You," said Bruce Martell with slow distinctness, "are a damned, crusty, pig-headed old catamount. For a long time you've been the big mogul around here, had this whole big chunk of country for your own back yard to play around in. That's made you proud. But down across the river now are hundreds of people, plenty of them damned fine people. Should you get 'em worked up to the necessary pitch, they could come across the river and rub you out like you were a lone ant on a hot rock. That's exactly what will happen one of these days if you try to live alongside 'em with a chip always on your shoulder. But if you make friends with enough of those people, they'll be good for you and you'll be good for them. As the set-up now stands, there's the fattest chunk of business you ever saw right here in front of you. Can't you see that?"

"I see what I like to look at, and do as I damned please," growled Asbell. "I never bowed my neck to any damned man, and I shore don't intend to start doing it now to a flock of sod-busters. They let me alone, I let them alone. But any time they want trouble, let 'em cut their wolf loose."

"Nobody is suggesting that you bow your neck to anybody," said Martell. "I'm just . . ."

"You're wasting your time and mine, friend," cut in Asbell again.

Martell took a final inhale, pinched out his cigarette butt. "When the Lord set out to make the most pig-headed critter in all creation, He made an old-line cattleman. To hell with you."

He stepped off the porch, went over to the black horse, and gathered up the reins. That was when a hard voice came across at him from the bunk-house door.

"Keep your hands full of reins . . . an' nothin' else, mister! This Winchester is lookin' right down your throat!"

Bruce went completely still, except for his head. He turned this and saw the rifle and the man behind it. And he saw Carp Bastion coming past the corner of the bunkhouse, a hard grin on his face. Carp didn't have a gun, but he was opening and closing his fists with anticipation.

Bruce's eyes, now cold and smoky, came back to Asbell. "What is this?" he rapped harshly.

"An idea of Carp's," answered Asbell, his eyes sardonic. "You've roughed Carp up a couple of times when you got the jump by surprise. Carp don't think you can do it again from an even start. You've got nothing worse ahead of you than a going-over with fists. Nobody else will mix in. But the idea is that you take your gun off before the roundelay starts."

"No need of throwing a Winchester against me if that's all you want," gritted Bruce. "Seems this whole damned outfit needs to be convinced of something or other." He ignored the poised rifle, dropped the rein, unbuckled his gun belt, and hung it to the saddle horn. He turned and moved to meet Bastion.

"All right, Carp. This is the third time. It's going to be the roughest on you."

Carp's grin didn't fade. He had a lot of confidence in his burly power and he'd seen more than one man go down under the lash of his knotted fists. He went into this with a headlong rush, fists flailing.

The world seemed to explode. And something hit him heavily across the flat of his shoulders. This was the earth.

Carp rolled over, got up, trying to get his eyes in focus again. It was as though a mule had kicked him on the side of the jaw. He hadn't seen that punch coming; he hadn't even seen it start. But he knew it had landed. He floundered a little, blinking, and located Martell again, standing poised and waiting.

"Better call it off, Carp," said Martell. "I've had a lot more experience at this sort of thing than you. I don't want to mess you up."

Carp did the only thing he knew how to do. He came in again, fists windmilling. Bruce side-stepped, cuffed him on the ear, grabbed him, swung him around, and belted him on the jaw again. Carp's knees wobbled, but he managed to stay up. He launched a wild swing that landed squarely on the bandaged wound on Bruce's left arm.

A gust of pain ran all through Bruce and he knew that the wound had broken open again. In fact, almost instantly there was a sogginess under the bandage and then a moist, warm seeping down his arm.

Bruce gave back, and Carp came on in, leaping at his momentary advantage. Bruce crouched under two whistling punches and then uppercut wickedly. Carp's head snapped back and he was wide open, arms waving. Bruce set himself and duplicated his first punch.

That finished it. Carp was on the ground again and, though he floundered blindly, he couldn't get up.

Bruce turned back to his horse, his glance raked Hack Asbell. "Everybody satisfied?" he rapped curtly.

Asbell was looking at Bruce's left hand, streaked with seeping crimson. "You didn't use the left hand once," said the cattleman. "But it's bleeding. How come?"

Bruce touched his arm. "A wound here, not healed. It broke open."

A queer look came over Asbell's face. "Why in hell didn't you say you had a wounded arm?" he burst out.

"Why should I?" retorted Bruce. "You wanted a fracas, didn't you?"

He buckled on his gun, stepped into the saddle, and rode away, a big man in the saddle, a very big man at that moment.

Carp crawled to the edge of the porch, pulling himself up on it, sat there with his dazed head in his hands. Hack Asbell's voice dripped sarcasm.

"Well, did you find out?"

"I found out," mumbled Carp. "My God! Can that guy hit! He's a man, that feller is, Hack."

"His left arm was wounded," lashed Asbell. "You broke it open. He was bleeding when he left."

"I didn't know that," groaned Carp. "Now I feel like a damned dog. A damned dog!" He got to his feet and lurched over to the bunkhouse. "He fought me fair and he licked me quick. He could 'a' cut me to ribbons, but he didn't. And him with a wounded arm." Carp's shame was abysmal.

Hack Asbell watched Bruce Martell out of sight, then threw his cheroot butt aside.

"Butte . . . Speck!" he yelled. "One of you saddle up a bronc' for me. I'm going to town."

He went back into the cabin, found his worn old Peacemaker Colt gun, and buckled it on. Then he went over to the corrals, where Butte was catching up a good-looking sorrel.

"Think you ought to, boss?" asked Butte, lanky and tow-headed.

"Ought to . . . what?" snapped Asbell.

"Ride into town. Plenty of feelin' against us down there right now. Better let some of us boys go in with you. Three or four of us together the sod-busters leave alone. But one man . . . !"

"Hell with the sod-busters!" growled Asbell. "For twenty years I been riding into Starlight whenever I felt like it, to have a couple of drinks with Sam Beardon across his bar, and deal a few hands of cards with him. Why should I change now, just because of a few sod-busters?"

"Not a few, boss," murmured Butte. "A lot. A hell of a lot."

Asbell's answer was just a snort. He waited until Butte had the sorrel ready, then went into the saddle. "You boys patrol the lower range again today," he ordered. "No telling when them cussed slow-elkers will try their luck again."

He shook the sorrel's reins and was gone.

Chapter Seven

It was in the warm hours of midafternoon when Bruce Martell rode into the town of Starlight again. He hadn't intended seeing this town of violent memories so soon again, but a circumstance had come up that made it necessary. At the urging of his brother Kip and Jeff Clebourne, Bruce had staked out a piece of land just upriver from their holdings. It was virtually an island, with an ancient overgrown channel cutting around to the south side of it. There was just about a quarter section in the chunk, and when Bruce finally consented to look it over with Kip, he found it a strangely attractive place.

It was walled off from the rest of the world by the river channels and borders of tall, cool alders and was of deep, rich soil. Bruce could conceive of little chance that he'd ever have use for it himself, not permanently, anyhow. But a man did not have to be sharp as a weasel to see how things definitely were between Kip and Cadence Clebourne. These two kids had star dust in their eyes. And later on, if all went well, an extra chunk of good land turned over to them wouldn't hurt their future any. And so Bruce had set his stakes and was now in town to record it at the Land Office.

Starlight did not seem so jammed-up as it had been before. Most of the wagons on the street were ponderous freighters, bringing in supplies to pour into the clamoring maw of this surging new country. Bruce kept off the street with the black, going around behind the store to leave the horse at the corral there. Then, wanting to pay his way out at the Clebourne camp, he went into the store, and when he finally got a turn at the counter, ordered up a couple of sides of bacon and a few luxury items that he thought might please Cadence Clebourne. He put this all in a sack that he carried around and tied behind the saddle of the black. Then he went over to the Land Office.

Here, also, the crush had thinned out and presently he was able to claim the attention of Cashel Edmunds, the agent, a tall, dark man with a hungry nose. Edmunds had a quick, soft way of moving about, and his eyes were sharp and questioning and none too friendly as he listened to Bruce supply the necessary description and data on his claim.

"What's Rocking A trying to do?" demanded Edmunds. "Edge back across the river, maybe?"

"What's Rocking A got to do with it?" asked Bruce. "I'm not riding for Asbell. Even if I was, it's none of your affair. I'm twenty-one, and a citizen of reasonable good standing. I got as much right to settle on a piece of free land as the next man. Suppose we get the filing done and let the talk go."

Their eyes locked and it was Edmunds who looked away. He made the necessary recordings and handed over the preliminary title claim.

"You've got to prove up the same as everybody else," snapped Edmunds. "You've got to . . ."

"I know all about that," cut in Bruce. "It'll be done."

He was turning to the door when he heard the first swelling growl of voices, down at the lower end of town, a growl that grew and harshened swiftly. He stepped to the door, with Edmunds at his shoulder.

A buckboard was coming up the street, its team of broncos at a walk. All about it surged a thickening crowd. Driving the wagon was a big man in corduroy coat and trousers. It was Jason Spelle, who Bruce had met that night at the Carling camp. Spelle was bareheaded, his hair tawny in the slanting sunlight. Some kind of word was shuttling through the crowd and men jostled and pushed and struggled, trying to get close enough to the buckboard to see what was lying across the narrow back of it. And all the time the fierce, gathering rumble of a savage anger lifted and grew.

At the outer edge of the crowd a man lifted a yell that cut through the clamor of the rest.

"Tell us about it, Jason . . . tell us about it!"

Almost directly in front of the Land Office, Jason Spelle drew his team to a halt. He stood up and looked around. He made a dominant, compelling figure, and when he held up his hand, the crowd quieted. His voice rolled, big and strong and bitter.

"I want every settler in Indio Basin to know about this. Jake Hendee lies dead in the back of this buckboard. Some of you may have known Jake, but, for those who didn't, I'm telling you that he was a good, law-abiding, honest man. Purely by chance I drove by his camp today. And what did I find? Why I found the pole of his wagon propped up and poor Jake Hendee with a rope around his neck, hanging to it! There was a sign pinned to his shirt . . . this sign. I'll read it to you!"

Spelle took a crumpled paper from his coat pocket, smoothed it out. The crowd became almost breathlessly still, every man leaning forward, not wanting to miss a single word.

"Here's what it says," boomed Spelle. " 'Warning! This is what will happen to every sod-buster found eating Rocking A beef!' "

Spelle swung his glance across the crowd and waved the paper. "That's what it says. Those are the exact words of it. They took Jake Hendee and lynched him to his own wagon pole. Murder! That's what it was . . . cowardly, ruthless murder. And we can thank Hack Asbell and the Rocking A for it."

The crowd, wild-eyed and seething, broke into a renewed roaring.

"Ah!" exclaimed Cashel Edmunds, at Bruce Martell's shoulder. "Now that damned high-handed, swaggering Rocking A outfit has done it! And if somebody in that crowd happens to remember that Hack Asbell rode into town today and is up at the hotel right now . . . this could turn into a very interesting afternoon."

At that moment someone in the crowd did remember and the word spread swiftly. The roar of voices deepened, took on an increasingly ugly note, and swept along the street toward the gaunt, two-story building at the upper end of town. A building that had stood in Starlight long before the first settler ever heard of Indio Basin—the Longhorn Hotel. Keeping pace with the crowd went Jason Spelle and his buckboard and the blanket-covered figure it carried. Cashel Edmunds said, a thin exultation in his voice: "I've got to see this. I'm locking up the office."

Bruce Martell did not follow Cashel Edmunds. Instead, he cut around in back of the Land Office, stayed well off the street, and circled at a run up to the rear of the hotel where, on a back porch, a rather blowzy-looking woman was scrubbing clothes in a battered galvanized tub.

She whipped stringy hair out of her eyes with a suds-covered hand, stared at Bruce, and asked: "What's all the racket about?"

"A fool and his talk," Bruce rapped. "Hack Asbell inside?"

"I reckon," the woman nodded. "What of it?"

Bruce didn't bother to answer. He went in, found himself in a kitchen, went out of it into a dining room with an oilcloth-covered table, cut through a side door into the hotel bar. Hack Asbell sat at a poker table and across from him was a fat, bald-headed man with a blocky face made round with rolls of loose flesh. The fat man had laid down his hand of cards and was staring toward the front of the hotel. If Hack Asbell heard the rumble of the crowd, he paid it no concern.

Bruce caught the cattleman by the shoulder. Asbell looked up, eyes widening.

"You again," he snorted. "What . . . ?"

"One question, Asbell," cut in Bruce. "Your crew . . . did they lynch a settler last night?"

"If they did, he was a slow-elker and had it coming. But they didn't, or I'd have known about it. What the devil are you driving at?"

"Never mind. Get out of here. Where's your horse?"

"Down at Joe Leggett's livery barn, taking on a feed of oats. Get out of here, you say? Are you crazy?"

"No. But you are if you don't get that stiffness out of your neck and listen to reason. My black horse is tied out back of the general store. If you sneak out of here the back way and circle wide, you can get to my bronc' without being seen. Then cut and run for it. Hurry up! You ain't got much time."

Hack Asbell pushed away from the table, stood up. His face was grim. "Now let's have it straight. What's the matter?"

"Matter enough. Hear that yelling outside?"

"I'm not deaf," Asbell snapped testily. "'Course I hear it. Damned crazy sod-busters. Always bellering and yapping over something. Let 'em howl. Nothing to me. Now what's this talk about my boys lynching . . . ?"

"The settlers got the body of one of their own kind out there. He was found hanging by the neck to a pole of his own wagon. There was a sign pinned on him, which said that any other settler found eating Rocking A beef would get the same treatment. That's a mob shaping up out there, Asbell. It's your hide they're yelling for. They want you, and they know you're in here. Will you get out of here and take my horse?"

Now that he fully understood, the grizzled cattleman went completely cool. He looked at Bruce gravely. "Son, you're going out of your way to help me. Why?"

Bruce shrugged desperately. "I don't know. Maybe because you're my kind of man. Maybe because I don't think you'd lie to me. And there's still another reason . . . my own."

A shrill, piercing voice cut through the solid clamor out in the street.

"Come on out, Asbell! Come on out or we come in after you. We got a rope just your size and length. Come on out!"

There wasn't a cowardly bone in Hack Asbell's spare, rawhide old carcass. He was a cattleman of the old school to whom vast acreages of unfenced range, with herds of cattle free to graze anywhere they willed, were badges of a sane, well-ordered world. He thought in terms of miles, not in quarter-sections. And he was afraid of nothing that walked.

"Son," he said, "the day I run from a flock of crazy sod-busters, that day I ain't fit to live. We'll just have a look at that gang and read the color of their hides."

He headed for the front door of the hotel, swearing to himself. The fat man spoke up quickly.

"No, Hack! Don't go out there. They'll eat you alive. Let me tell 'em off. This is my hotel and no man enters it without my permission."

While he spoke, the fat man was scurrying around behind the bar. He came up with a sawed-off shotgun, ancient and rusty. "They take a look down the throat of this," he puffed, "they'll think twice about busting into my place."

He would have gone to the door ahead of Asbell, but the cattleman pushed him back.

"No, Sam . . . you stay out of it. This is my

steak to chaw. Appreciate it, of course . . . but I don't need your help. That crowd wants a look at me and I won't disappoint 'em."

In another stride he was through the door and out on the hotel porch. The hoarse howl that greeted his appearance washed menacingly against the sky. In the vanguard of the crowd was Jason Spelle and his wagon, drawn up just beyond the porch steps.

Hack Asbell stood, feet slightly spread, looking out over the yelling, threatening mass of settlers with an iron-jawed defiance. The clamor of the crowd beat against the front of the hotel in waves of sound. Asbell waited, motionless, for them to quiet.

Watching the old cattleman, Bruce Martell knew stirring admiration. Here was steel-cold nerve, bitter and defiant. In his time, Bruce Martell had seen men with more than an average share of courage go pale and sweating in the face of mob wrath, and this was definitely mob wrath now, with numbers steadily augmented all the time. But Hack Asbell was as solid and unmoved and as coldly indifferent as if he'd been carved in stone.

"A lot of man," mumbled Sam Beardon, the fat hotelkeeper. "Old Hack is a lot of man. I'll kill somebody before I see that mob take hold of him."

The mob quieted enough for his words to carry, so Hack Asbell hurled his defiance flatly.

"Well, here I am! You wanted to see me. Take a good look. What's all this howling about a rope cut to my size?"

"The same size and length of the one you hung Jake Hendee on!" bawled a settler, and this set off another massed roar. Again Asbell waited for their clamor to die.

"I know nothing about a Jake Hendee being lynched, and neither does my outfit. The only ones we're out to lynch are the damned slow-elkers who've been butchering my stock. We catch any of them and they'll be lynched, all right . . . and I'll invite you to the party. But so far we ain't had any luck. That's my word on it!"

They howled at him again, and the rising hate was like a macabre heat.

Now it was Jason Spelle who took over, waving his arms to quiet the mob. He was standing up in his wagon and he pointed a dramatic arm at Asbell.

"It won't do you any good to lie, Asbell. I know what I found, and I know how the sign on Hendee's body read. If you wanted your murderous warning to carry all over Indio Basin, you've succeeded better than you know. You've done something else. You've aroused the avenging wrath of a peaceable, long-suffering people. Now you must answer to that just wrath!"

It was overdone, it was sticky, it was cheap melodrama, but it suited the mood of the mob perfectly. There came an ominous forward crowding, a flowing of insensate power, blind and ravening. Hack Asbell met it with harsh words that ripped out like bullets.

"Why, you big-mouthed, forked-tongued whelp! Calling me a liar . . . spreading that kind of mealy-lipped talk. Get out of that wagon and come up here where I can get my hands on you!"

Bruce Martell, watching closely from the hotel door, saw Cashel Edmunds standing beside Spelle's buckboard. He saw Edmunds turn and say something to a man standing beside him. The fellow spread his arms to make room, the threw a fist-sized rock straight at Hack Asbell's head.

The missile flew true. It landed with a crunching thud. Hack Asbell crumpled in a heap. Instantly the mob started forward, whining its eagerness to lay hands on the unconscious cattleman.

They never got there, for Bruce Martell arrived first. A hand clawing at Asbell was kicked aside savagely, and the owner of it fell back, cursing the agony of a broken wrist. Then Bruce Martell was blocking the way, a tall, bleak-faced figure with cold, bitter eyes, and with a drawn gun in his hand. His voice rang.

"I'll kill the first man to put a foot on this porch! Or the next one to throw a brickbat. You, Spelle . . . call 'em off!"

At first glance the mob saw only another man

up there on the porch, facing them. Then they saw something else. It was something invisible, but real. It was an indefinite atmosphere of authority, which came out of him in a chill, unyielding current. It was a thing made up of background, of past experience in the ways of violent deeds and violent men. It was as real as if a star of office were pinned on him. Here, they realized, was a man who had faced mobs before, who knew the uselessness of verbal argument with one, but who knew perfectly the one type of argument any mob could not fail to recognize. Force—and a ready deadly gun to back it up with.

He had proclaimed a deadline—the edge of the porch. And not a man in that mob but understood Martell stood ready to do exactly what he threatened—which was to kill the first one who tried to cross that deadline. They hated him for it, they raged against him, but they obeyed him. No one of them tried to come up on the porch.

Jason Spelle alone seemed to believe that Bruce Martell could be bluffing. At any rate he again produced the inflammatory notice and waved it in an attempt to whip them to fresh fury.

"I told you what was written on this!" he shouted. "Jake Hendee was one of us. I told you . . . !"

The hard, coughing blast of a gun cut through Spelle's tirade. Part of the paper he was waving, sheared off by an accurate slug, fluttered and drifted downward. A thin haze of smoke curled from the muzzle of Martell's gun and his voice whipped out again.

"Last warning, Spelle! Shut that big yap of yours and get out of here. I mean . . . you!"

From behind Martell, Sam Beardon's fat man's voice wheezed. "Buckshot in both barrels of this. It'll spread and take in plenty. You can have all of it if you want!"

Jason Spelle stared at the fragment of paper still in his grasp. Then he swung his head and stared at Bruce Martell. His eyes paled with a baffled, white-hot rage. Over stiff lips he spoke just three words.

"We'll be back!"

Then he faced the mob once more, waved a commanding arm down the street, caught up the reins, and urged his team to movement. The moving buckboard broke up the hard pack of the mob and men fell in behind it, following it, sending their confused anger back in growls and fading curses. Soon there was open space before the steps. Bruce Martell leaned down, caught Hack Asbell under the arms, and dragged him inside.

Chapter Eight

Blue twilight smoked up the world, cooling only what a man could see with his eyes and feel with his hand. Beyond that, the town of Starlight seethed and boiled with the angers and passions of men. To a listening ear the town hummed like a hive of disturbed bees. It was a sound made up of the voices of many men, walking up and down the street, massing at saloon bars and in front of Donovan's store. There were no shrill and solitary yelps or shouts, the venting of individual anger, but just that ominous, growing hum, intensifying with every passing minute. It held a significance to make a man's nerves crawl.

In the Longhorn Hotel, Bruce Martell prowled back and forth, having his look and his moments of listening at all sides. All the weight of past experience told him that Jason Spelle had meant what he said. They would be back. It was forming out there now, the purpose and the power. It would come after dark, sometime during the night. The tide had washed up as far as the hotel porch steps, then ebbed back, a wave that had not had quite enough power to engulf. But when it came again . . .

There was a light burning in the Land Office and a buckboard standing in front of the place—Jason

Spelle's buckboard. Spelle himself was in the Land Office, along with Cashel Edmunds. Watching at a hotel window, Bruce Martell saw men constantly passing in and out of the lit doorway. Listening, he heard wagons pounding out of town, but more wagons coming back. And so he could guess what was going on. The word was being spread. The ghost of Jake Hendee was being dangled in settler camps everywhere, as bait for the gullible. And the gullible were pouring into town, to give added weight to Jason Spelle's promise. *We'll be back!*

There were just four people in the hotel. Bruce Martell, Hack Asbell, Sam Beardon, and the blowzy woman who had been washing clothes, and who was Sam Beardon's cook and maid-of-all-work about the hotel. Beardon and the woman were working over Asbell, who was stretched on an ancient sofa in the hotel parlor. Martell, after still another prowl around through the hotel, stopped in there.

"How is he?" he asked.

"Scares me," mumbled Sam Beardon. "Got his eyes open, but don't seem to see anything. He's conscious, yet he ain't conscious. He's here, but he's somewhere else, too."

"Concussion," murmured Martell. "Which doesn't make it any easier. Sam, we got to get him out of here. They're going to come again. They've sent out messengers to spread the word.

In a couple of hours from now there'll be three times as many settlers in town as we had to face this afternoon. Some of them will be liquored up. It'll take more than just the sight of a gun or two to turn 'em back. Yeah, we got to get Asbell out of here."

"How're we going to do it?" asked Beardon. "Right now he couldn't sit a saddle, even if we had one for him. Which we ain't. Hack allus leaves his bronc' at Joe Leggett's livery barn. It's down there now and, things being like they are, it might jest as well be a thousand miles from here. And they got watchers strung all around this damn' hotel."

"I'll get him out," said Martell grimly, "if I have to shoot my way through every settler in the basin. There's a lot of things in the air I don't savvy, but I'm sure of one thing. Asbell's too good a man to die on the end of a rope. I've got a couple of ideas. Here's what you do, Sam. Get a light going in a front, upstairs room. You and the lady act plenty busy in that room, moving back and forth between the window and the light. Be carrying towels, a basin of water. Make it look like you got an injured man in that room you're tending to. I'll show a couple of times in the room myself. They'll be watching and they'll think we got Asbell in there. And then, when the dark settles in, good and thick, I'll take Asbell out the back way."

"You'll have to carry him, and you can't carry him far," argued Beardon. "Besides, they got watchers out back."

"A couple." Martell nodded. "With a little luck, I'll take care of them. We've got to take the chance, Sam. It's the only way."

The fat man was still for a moment, looking down at his old friend, Hack Asbell. Slowly he nodded. "All right." And so the things Martell suggested were done. The false show was put on in the upstairs room, and Martell, lingering once by the open window of the room, knew that at least some of the effect he had gambled on had gone over. For he heard a man down in the now-black street call to another.

"See that, Cass? They're puttin' Asbell to bed. That rock must've hit plenty hard. Tell Spelle we're liable to find ourselves tryin' to lynch a dead man."

"Dead or alive, just so we lynch him," came the answer.

Martell drifted to the door of the room. Sam Beardon looked at him. "Good luck!"

The blowzy woman, softening under the strain, began to snivel and dabbed at her nose.

Martell went down to the parlor. He did not try to get Asbell to his feet. He simply lifted the old cattleman in his arms and carried him back through the darkened hotel to the rear door. He laid Asbell down on the kitchen floor, edged the door open, looked and listened. The night out here was still. But somewhere out here were men posed to watch. Before full dark had come down, he'd located two of them, one at each back corner of the hotel. He couldn't be sure that's where they were now, or whether there were more than two by this time. But the die was cast. It was this way or no way. He went out and across the ancient porch, moving as softly as he could. The last of the porch steps let out a protesting squeak as he moved off it. A voice struck sharply at him from the dark.

"Who is it?"

He turned toward the voice, moving steadily. He answered in heavy, muffled tones. "Who do you think? Spelle told me to make a circle and see if everything was quiet back here. Looks like they've put Asbell to bed upstairs, but you never can tell. . . ."

His eyes probed the dark with straining intentness. He located the man, a vague shadow, standing at the corner of the building ahead of him. He slid his gun noiselessly free and kept on moving in.

"We shouldn't have let 'em bluff us out in the first place," he went on, in that same muffled way. "The time to have stretched Asbell was when we had him down and out. . . ."

Now he was close enough, and he moved with explosive speed. He leaped, his gun chopping out and down. A yell of startled alarm formed in the throat of the man in front of him, but before it could erupt, Martell's gun thudded home. The man grunted and went down.

Swift and complete as this thing had been, still it left some small sound. Any violence was that way; it could never be completely noiseless. For even though the ear could not hear it, it seemed to throw out invisible waves that a man could feel. And now, from the other rear corner of the hotel, a man called.

"Hocken! Oh, Hocken! What's going on over there? You hear anything? Who's that you were talking to?"

Martell walked straight back toward the speaker. "Just checking up," he said. "Spelle and Edmunds want to make sure the bird don't get away. Spelle said to tell you fellers to watch that back door."

It got him most of the way there, but he was still several feet short when the guard's indecision became open alarm. Martell moved as fast as he ever had in his life, but he still didn't get there in time to beat the hoarse yell that the fellow lifted. Right after that, Martell got him with his lashing gun barrel.

Martell turned, raced for the kitchen door. He brought Asbell up off the floor, jack-knifed him over his shoulder. Then he plunged out into the night again, running. He headed straight away into the open country beyond the edge of town, and when he got a hundred yards of darkness behind him, he began to circle.

Back at the hotel men were shouting. There was a high and angry cursing when someone stumbled over one of the guards Martell had gun whipped. Panting heavily from the violence of this physical effort he was putting out, Martell knew cold exultation.

Let 'em cuss . . . let 'em yell. They'd be like chickens with their heads cut off for a few precious minutes, bumbling and thrashing around, mired down in their own confusion. Most men were like that. Surprise, the bewilderment of things unexpected, turned them inside out. They'd do a lot of senseless charging here and there, but unless the scent was red hot or the trail plain under their noses, they'd waste a great deal of time doing a great deal of nothing. And this night was big and dark.

Martell stopped to rest. His heart was pounding, breath rasped in and out of him in hungry gulps. Across his shoulder Hack Asbell hung loose as a sack, yet groaning a little.

Martell went on, sighting the indistinct masses of the town buildings to his right. The hotel was easy to distinguish. And Donovan's store was about—there! He drifted in, slowed now to a walk. He had the line he wanted.

He lowered Hack Asbell to the black earth, and

spoke, though he knew Asbell did not hear him.

"I'll be back after you, Hack."

Relieved of the cattleman's weight, he was his old, soft-moving, swift-prowling self. He came up to the corral in back of Donovan's store. And then knew a relief so great it was almost a tide of weakness. The black horse was there, just as he'd left it. He mauled the horse's head and ears for a happy moment, then freed the reins, and led it away at a walk.

In back of him the town was surging with the alarm. But what could they be sure of? A pair of hotel guards found gun whipped and unconscious. How much else could they guess and what definitely could they be sure of? Who was still in the hotel and who wasn't? Later they'd find out, but for the moment . . .

Martell laughed softly as he drew the black to a stop beside Hack Asbell's prone figure. The sack of food he had tied behind the saddle earlier that day, he now loosened and tossed aside. The black would have enough to carry without that. He got Hack Asbell across the saddle, then swung up behind. And then he rode deeper and deeper into the wide night.

Chapter Nine

It was full midnight when the black horse breasted the slope of the flat below the Rocking A headquarters, moving slowly and wearily, for the miles had been long under a double burden.

There were no lights about the place, and when Martell pulled up beside the corrals, he lifted his call.

"Carp! Oh, Carp!"

He had to call again before there came a stirring in the bunkhouse, a rumble of voices, and then a stir at the door of the building.

"Who's out there . . . who's yellin' for me?"

"Your old friend, Martell. The man on the black horse. Get some lights going. I got Hack Asbell here, and he's hurt."

This word cleaned the bunkhouse in a hurry. They came running, half dressed, and Carp Bastion had a lantern. They crowded around and threw the lantern light on Martell and Hack Asbell.

"You!" blurted Carp. "The boss . . . what's wrong with him?"

"A dirty wallop on the head," explained Martell tersely. "Tell you all about it, later. Right now we got to get Hack comfortable as possible. He's on a slippery trail. Easy, now. Watch his head."

There were plenty of brawny arms to cradle the old cattleman and carry him into his cabin. Martell stepped down, stamped the stiffness from his legs, and followed them in. Hack Asbell lay still on his bunk, his grim face drawn, his eyes closed. The bandage that the woman at the hotel had put on his head was still in place. They pulled off his boots, undressed him, got him between blankets. Then they faced Martell.

"Tell us," they said grimly.

Martell gave them the story. Carp Bastion cursed harshly. "Those damn' crazy sod-busters. We never hung that feller, Hendee. We never did nothin' but go through a few camps, lookin' for slow-elked beef. That Jason Spelle *hombre* is the world's biggest liar. I'm gonna ride up on that guy and . . ."

"The point is," broke in Martell, "that you boys didn't lynch Hendee. But somebody did. And they left a sign on him pointing at Rocking A. The more you think on that angle, the bigger and uglier it gets."

"Old Hack," said one of the other riders. "He needs a doctor. And there never was one in Starlight. Where . . . ?"

"A doctor couldn't do much more for him than we can do," said Martell. "If that rock caved Hack's head, he's done for, doctor or no doctor. But I don't believe it did. But he has got a concussion. And the thing that'll straighten that out is complete quiet and rest. Give him a few hours, just as he is, and we'll have a pretty good idea."

Butte Allen said: "Then let's get out of here to do our palavering. Muley, get your fire going in the cook shack and brew up some coffee. We'll do our talking in there."

Which was what they did. They gathered around the long cook shack table, drank hot coffee, and had their say. Butte Allen fixed Martell with grimly questioning eyes.

"Why did you side Hack?" he demanded. "What was it to you whether the sod-busters lynched him, or not?"

"For one thing, I like the old man," said Martell simply. "I like the layer of salt along his backbone. Again, I don't like mobs. I don't like that guy, Spelle, who was leading the settlers. And then, a man always has a feeling for his own kind of people. I don't agree with some of Hack's ideas, as you know, but he's a cowman, and my kind." He shrugged. "There were a lot of reasons."

"Come mornin'," said Carp Bastion savagely, "we'll saddle up and ride, and scatter sod-busters all over the prairie."

"No you won't, Carp," said Martell. "The outfit stays right here at headquarters until Hack Asbell gets well enough to have another long talk with me. After that, we'll see."

"You got your damn' nerve," blurted Carp. "Who are you to tell us what we do?"

105

"I'm the guy who brought Hack Asbell home, Carp. I got him out of that mess . . . you didn't. He'd have been kicking on air long before this, but for me. I'm not bragging or asking for thanks or any of that sort of thing. But there's an angle there that gives me a big say in things, whether you can see it or not. For once, use your head. I don't want a fourth tangle with you. I'd rather shake hands and call it square. Can't any of the rest of you see what I'm driving at?"

Butte Allen nodded slowly. "I see it. Carp, Martell here is right. We sit tight."

Carp, pugnacious, intolerant, stared at Martell. Then, slowly, he grinned and put out his hand.

"You win. I'm the guy who don't want any fourth tangle with you. Last time you beat my ears off. My jaw still feels lop-sided. You could have murdered me without half tryin'. I don't know where you learned to fight that way, but I want no more of it. Quits it is, Martell."

In the first warming touch of a new day's sunlight, Hack Asbell looked better. The pulled tautness of his face had softened and his color was better. He was sleeping quietly.

In the bunkhouse, Martell got some sleep himself. At noon Carp Bastion shook him awake. "Hack's come out of it and is askin' for you."

Martell went into the cabin, grinned down at Asbell, who gave back a grim smile. The cattleman's voice was not quite up to normal strength, but it was clear and steady.

"Carp's been telling me how I got here. Thanks, son. I never even saw the damned rock that hit me. Must be getting soft-headed in my old age to go out and stay out like I done. What do you make of it all?"

Martell pulled up a chair, built a smoke. "Rocking A didn't lynch that Jake Hendee. But somebody did. So we start from there. Why did they lynch him and why did they put that lying sign on him?"

Hack Asbell squinted his eyes. "Only one answer to that, I reckon. Somebody wants to get the sod-busters hating me and my outfit mortal bad."

"That's the obvious answer," agreed Martell. "There could be some more. But we'll stay with the first one for a while. Hack, I wish you'd listen to reason. Like I told you before, there are some mighty fine people down in that basin. I've got a brother down there, tying in with one settler family. It's a fine break for the kid, something he's needed. The settler he's with, Jeff Clebourne . . . he's the kind of a man you could sit down with, swap ideas, and be happy to call your friend. There's another family I met . . . the Carlings . . . well, they don't come any better. You need folks like that for friends, Hack . . . and you can have 'em as friends if you'll just open your mind and be practical about things."

"Huh," grunted Asbell. "I can see where you're heading. Still want me to sell beef to them sod-busters, don't you?"

"That's one angle," Martell admitted. "It would help things a lot. You only get back from people what you bring to them, Hack. Indio Basin needs fresh beef. The settlers will get it from you, or from somebody else. You show 'em you're willing to do business with them, and I know they'll meet you more than halfway. And it would put a damper on this slow-elking that's been in your hair. Of course, you know Donovan who runs the general store in Starlight?"

"Sure I know him. Good man, if the sod-busters don't spoil him."

"You could work out a beef deal through him. Let him peddle it to the settlers. Good business for you, good for him. And good will toward you on the part of the decent settlers. You admit that Hendee's lynching points to someone who was out to get every settler in the basin to hate your guts. Here's a chance to fight back with something more worthwhile and enduring than guns."

"You'd talk a man out of his lone pair of pants," growled Asbell irritably. "Get me a cheroot outta that box yonder. I want to think."

Martell got the cheroot and scratched a match. Asbell puffed furiously. "All right," he agreed suddenly. "On one condition. You ride for me. You take over as foreman. You take Carp's place. Carp won't mind too much. You licked him, fair and clean. That makes you a better man than him, in Carp's eyes. And you *are* a better man. You think with your head. All Carp uses his for is to bump it into things. A deal?"

Martell took a turn around the room, stopped, and looked down at the grizzled cattleman.

"You don't know much about me, Hack. You don't . . ."

"I know all I need to know. A man's got it the first time you meet him, or he ain't. Time's got nothing to do with it. That damned rock pounded something into my head. It made me realize I ain't as young as I used to be. It made me see that, like you said the other day, the world moves on and things change. I'd be a dead man right now, but for you, son. Damn it all . . . I like you, and I want you with me. How about it?"

Martell was gravely still for another moment.

"Now who's being bull-headed stubborn?" asked Asbell plaintively.

The breaking smile warmed Bruce Martell's face. He put out his hand. "It's a deal, Hack."

"Swell! Great! There's a bottle hid in that corner yonder. Get it. A drink is just what I need."

After they both took a swig, Martell slapped the cork back into the pint. "Who's to tell Carp?"

"You're foreman, ain't you? You tell him."

Martell said: "All right. I may not see you again until tomorrow. When I do, I want to see you right where you are . . . in that bunk. That's an order."

"Huh? You don't need to bully me. Couldn't get up if I wanted to. I'm still shaky as a new-born, bald-faced calf. Watch yourself, son."

Hack Asbell stared at the doorway for a little while after Martell left.

"Son," he murmured, wistfulness in his eyes. "Why does it come so easy for me to call him that? I could have used one like him."

Out at the corrals, Martell drew Carp Bastion aside and told him of the agreement he'd reached with Hack Asbell. "I hope it ain't going to make a bit of difference between you and me, Carp."

Carp was still for a minute, then his grin came. "You licked me, didn't you? That makes you top dog. Think I'll be happier this way. Fact is, I know I will. And I'll back your hand from here to China, cowboy."

"Now," said Martell gruffly, "I know why I've been liking you better all the time."

Chapter Ten

At the Clebourne camp, Martell was greeted with open relief. Kip covered his feelings with gruffness.

"Where the devil you been? I've been fit to tie, what with all the rumor flying around. Feller came by with the word that the Rocking A had lynched a settler named Jake Hendee. That was yesterday evening. Then, this morning we heard that Hack Asbell had been cornered in town and about to be strung up in payment for Hendee, but that he got away because a guy answering your description helped him. What's the truth of things?"

Bruce gave them the story and watched the frown deepen on Jeff Clebourne's face. Bruce headed off the settler's obvious thoughts.

"The Rocking A positively did not lynch Hendee, Mister Clebourne. But somebody did."

"Which means . . . what?" growled Clebourne.

"It could mean that somebody is out to make suckers of the settlers in this basin, to point the finger at Rocking A for some shady purpose of their own. Who that person or persons may be, or what their purpose is, I don't know. But I'm going to try and find out. Men like you can help."

"How?"

"By being a steadying influence. By advising the less thoughtful settlers, the more excitable and easily led ones not to jump at conclusions. That mob business that Jason Spelle was trying to stir up could have led to something very bad. It could have put dead men all up and down the street in Starlight. What do you know about Spelle?"

"Nothing much. He gets around a lot. Mighty popular with the settlers . . . always doing somebody a good turn. Met up with the man a couple of times. Seemed a pretty decent sort to me."

Bruce did not press the question. He looked at Cadence, who stood between her father and Kip, big-eyed and silent.

"Had a sack of grub for camp in town last night, youngster." He smiled. "Also a couple of surprises for you. Had to leave it when I lugged Asbell out on my horse. Next time I'll bring it, sure."

She had a grave, intent way of studying a man. Now she smiled back shyly. "Just so you got out of that affair all right," she said. "You had us worried."

"Lesson one. Never worry about me. I generally land on my feet."

"You've got a look about you," observed Kip. "When you first rode in, there was nothing in your eyes beyond the satisfaction of locating me. Now there's something else. Like a day in that camp of Rawhide when you walked down the street to break up a ruckus between a flock of miners and muleskinners. You wore a badge, but that was a small part of it. There was something else, something that made you ten feet high and wagon wide across the shoulders. You've got the same look, now. The old fires are burning, ain't they? I know."

Gravity settled Bruce's features again. "There's something loose in this basin, kid. I don't know what it is, but it's not good."

He let it go at that, turning to his horse. He tipped his hand as he rode off. "I'll be around, every now and then."

"Strange man, your brother is, Kip," murmured Jeff Clebourne. "And he has got that look about him. Plenty big in the saddle, right now."

"Somebody," said Kip, "is in for an awful rough ride. I know old Bruce. Even when I was a little bit of a kid, he was that way. When there was a mean chore to be done, Bruce did it. If a bully needed being worked down to size, Bruce worked him. If there was a mean bronc' to be topped, Bruce was the one who stepped into the saddle. It ain't that he likes to throw his weight around, because he don't. It's just that there's something in him . . . call it a strong sense of elemental justice, maybe. Anyhow, it's there. Take ramrodding the law, for instance. Most men in that game justwork at it as a chore. But Bruce was born to it. When he packs a star, it fills the street."

"There's no law in this basin now," said Clebourne.

"No," admitted Kip. "But it's on its way. And yonder rides the man most liable to put it there."

Chapter Eleven

There was a small room in back of the Land Office where Cashel Edmunds did his sleeping. Behind its locked door, four men sat. Cashel Edmunds, Jason Spelle, Pitch Horgan, and one known only as Brazos. The last was a hardcase, and looked it. He had a broken nose, bracketed by little, lead-colored eyes. It was dusky in the room, and warm, for the single window was closed and the shade drawn.

"All right, Brazos," growled Horgan. "Tell 'em."

There was a whiskey bottle on the table, and some heavy glasses. Brazos poured one of these nearly full, and sighted it against the crack of sunlight at the edge of the window shade, as though to savor it with his eyes before he did with his tongue. He had a voice as rough as his physical appearance, with a somewhat guttural run to it.

"This Bruce Martell *hombre* is poison . . . nothin' less. I know. I seen him work."

"Where?" asked Jason Spelle.

"Ravensdale. A tough camp. An awful tough camp. Wide open and with a tough ring runnin' things. But the ring got greedy. They weren't satisfied with the usual pickin's from their dives. They got to buyin' high-grade off the miners.

That's when the mine owners stepped in. They hired Martell to marshal the town and dry up that market for high-grade. He dried it up . . . plenty."

Spelle stirred restlessly. "He's only one man. He don't stand so tall."

Brazos gulped his whiskey, wiped a hairy, grimy wrist across his lips.

"How tall was he when he stood over Hack Asbell up on the hotel porch and made you and that mob of sod-busters back down, Spelle? I wasn't here to see it, but I heard tell of it. I heard he stood plenty tall, damn' near as tall as the sky. How about it?"

Spelle flushed and his eyes burned, pale and marble hard. "Those damn' settlers weren't quite ripe enough for a rush."

Brazos laughed hoarsely.

"I've heard them who backed down in front of him in Ravensdale make other excuses damn' near as good as that one. Let's not try and kid ourselves. This Bruce Martell has got something. I ain't got it, you ain't got it. But he has. It's something that rings a bell in you when you meet up with it, and the bell rings slow, like at a funeral. Your funeral. So you pull in your ears and duck. That's me. I want no part of Bruce Martell. Not any."

Cashel Edmunds spoke, thinly sarcastic. "Horgan, I thought you said this fellow Brazos was tough."

The glass Brazos held splintered on the floor as he dropped it. Then he was around the small table, had Cashel Edmunds by the shoulders, and was hauling him bodily out of his chair. He ran Edmunds backward across the room, slammed him against a wall, and held him there, his left hand jammed hard up under Edmunds's chin.

"Now what do you think, mister?" he snarled. "I'm plenty tough enough to twist the neck of a damn' slippery snake like you. I don't see you offerin' to brace Martell. Who are you to talk?"

"Take your dirty hands off him, Brazos! You hear me!"

It was Jason Spelle. There was a gun in his hand, the muzzle bearing on the center of Brazos thick body.

Brazos stepped away, still snarling. Edmunds dropped down on his bunk, his hands rubbing his throat.

"Let's get something straight and clear right now, once and for all," said Spelle. "Cashel and me are running this show. We give the orders. Horgan, you and the others do as you're told. That was our first understanding, that's the way it stays. Play along and there's plenty in this for all of us. Try and double-cross Cashel and me, or try and get out of line, and you'll wish you'd never been born. Let's understand that, finally and for good. Do we?"

Jason Spelle's face was suddenly as beaked and

116

cruel as that of a bird of prey. His eyes held a glitter.

"We'll play along," muttered Horgan. "But the boys will feel better when they see the pay-off for that first job. Brazos, sit down and stay down!"

"The pay-off will be as agreed," said Spelle. "A third to you. You'll have it in your pocket when you leave town tonight. But we were talking about this Bruce Martell. You feel about him the way Brazos does?"

Horgan stirred restlessly. "Only met up with him once in my life and I didn't know who he was, then. It was out at that sod-buster camp along the river when I was trying to run down that brother of his. Brazos is right. The man's got something about him that slows you up. I'm no coward, but I don't mind putting it this way. I'd either have to have a big edge, or there'd have to be plenty of chips on the table before I asked to see his smoke."

Jason Spelle's lips thinned, but he nodded, knowing he had received an honest answer from a tough man not given to easy fears. "We'll let that particular issue stand for a while. We'll admit the man is dangerous. But he's mortal. I'll think up another angle. Now we got other business to arrange. It will be tomorrow night. The fellow's name is Dopkins. I've reason to believe it will be a richer drag than the last one. I'll meet you at the regular place and point out the camp to you."

"You aim to leave another sign on this one?" asked Horgan.

"Not the same kind of a sign, but one that won't be mistaken. We'll arrange that when you leave town tonight. Now for the pay-off on the first job. Cash, get that money out of your safe."

As Edmunds moved to obey, Spelle poured himself a short drink. "The fools talk and tell me their plans. Which tells me how deep their sock is. A hundred thousand of that kind of money lying around, maybe more. Who knows? And in back of that the Rocking A. Beef to be sold to them, hungry for it. Thousands of dollars' worth. Stick with me, Pitch, and we'll all be rich. Once in a man's lifetime this kind of a chance comes along. It's right in our laps. We can't miss. Here's luck!"

Chapter Twelve

Pat Donovan was a chunky, florid-faced Irishman with keen blue eyes that twinkled easily, but shrewdly. He faced Bruce Martell across the width of his little cubby of an office in a rear corner of his store.

"And now, Mister Martell," he said. "What would this bit of business be?"

"Fresh beef," Bruce told him. "If you had any of it, could you sell it?"

"Could I sell it? Man! The settlers are crying for it. But mind you now, I'll have nothing to do with any but honest beef. There is talk of slow-elking being done against Hack Asbell's critters, and I don't like that. I don't like it at all."

"Neither do I, Mister Donovan," said Bruce. "But this is an honest deal. Rocking A beef, but on the square. Hack Asbell is ready to make a deal with you for all the beef you can sell. We would slaughter it and haul it in to you in dressed sides."

"We? You're riding for old Hack, Mister Martell? I thought I knew all of Hack's boys."

"I'm ramrodding for Hack now," explained Bruce. "He insisted on it that way."

The storekeeper studied Bruce keenly for a moment. Then he nodded. "You did a job of it, getting old Hack away from that mob of settlers. That was bad business and Jason Spelle should have known better, which I told him. I don't believe, and I will not, that Rocking A hung Jake Hendee. That was a dirty affair, and while Hack Asbell is a tough old codger, there is no meanness in the man. Should Hack ever have cause to lynch a man, then he would do it in the open, tell the world he had done it, and give his good reasons. But he is not the sort to murder a man in the dark. So you are his new foreman, eh? Knowing old Hack, I'd say you had to do a deal of talking to bring him to agreeing to this beef deal. Or am I guessing wrong, Mister Martell?"

Bruce's slow smile broke. "He took a mite of convincing, for a fact. Then you want that beef?"

Pat Donovan was emphatic. "I want it. But I must fix me up a cooling room and let the word get about that the beef is here. We will start easy and then keep up with the demand. And the prices will be fair?"

"Fair to Hack, fair to you, fair to the settlers," said Bruce. "We'll let you decide that angle, for you've the knowledge in such things."

Donovan rubbed his hands. "It will be good business all around," he declared. "Day after tomorrow I will be ready for three carcasses, Mister Martell."

"The beef will be here, bright and early in the

morning of that day," Bruce promised. "And it wouldn't hurt if with every chunk of beef you sell, you remind the buyer that it is honest Rocking A beef, sold to him at a fair price. It may get Rocking A some good will, which we can use."

"Aye!" agreed Donovan. "I see what you mean. I will spread the good word as far as I can, for there is need of good will in this basin and a gathering of fair minds and stout hearts." The storekeeper's tone had gone abruptly very grave.

Bruce swung an alert head. "You've a meaning behind that, Mister Donovan. What is it?"

"It is what a settler by the name of Otten was telling me," said Donovan slowly. "Otten knew Jake Hendee very well. They were neighbors back in a more settled country before deciding to come into Indio Basin in the land rush. And back there Jake Hendee had a very fair little property that he sold out when he left. Otten did not know the exact price Hendee got for his property, but his guess is that it would be perhaps fifteen or sixteen thousand dollars. Hendee brought that money with him to Indio Basin. Otten was sure of that from some remarks Hendee dropped. But when Otten and some other reliable settlers went over Hendee's camp to care for his effects, they found no penny of money. Though they did find a trunk in Hendee's wagon with the lock smashed. Did I say Jake Hendee's killing was a dirty business, Mister Martell?"

Bleak gravity pulled Bruce Martell's face into harsh lines. "This fellow Otten . . . he's reliable?"

"I would judge him so. A fair, upstanding sort who looks you in the eye. There are many such in this basin, but it would seem there are some rascals, too."

"Could you get Otten and some more of his kind together in this store by tonight, so I could talk to them? The more of them the better."

"I think that could be done," Donovan said.

"And leave out . . . Jason Spelle and Cashel Edmunds?"

Donovan started slightly, met Bruce's eyes for a long moment. "Now I wonder," said the store-keeper slowly, "if there isn't a deeper shrewdness in you than I dreamed. You stir up thoughts in me that I've been afraid to consider before. What have you to go on, man?"

"Virtually nothing, Pat," admitted Bruce. "Yet, things do not just happen in the affairs of men. The things men do are seldom without motive. I distrust self-appointed messiahs, and I don't like men who urge other men to throw rocks from the security of a mob. And sometimes, when you startle a man enough, the curtain lifts so that you see things beyond it that he'd rather keep hidden. You total these things up and, while you don't necessarily get a whole answer, you do get something to make you wonder. Which may not make sense to you."

"Ah, but it does," asserted Donovan. "So tonight we will leave out Jason Spelle and Cashel Edmunds."

"I'll be here about ten o'clock, after the town has quieted," promised Bruce.

The tide of settlers flowing in and out of Starlight was an ever-changing one. If any who saw Bruce Martell arrive at and leave Donovan's store were part of the mob that had clamored for Hack Asbell's neck, they did not show it openly. Nothing worse than the usual growls and sullen glances came his way.

Heading out, Bruce took a route he had traveled before. It led by Ezra Banks's camp, where the gaunt old settler was squaring up some foundations for a cabin. Ezra was not alone. Sitting, cross-legged, in the shade of Ezra's wagon, laying out something on a couple of tin plates on a square of tarpaulin, was Tracy Carling. She looked up as Bruce jogged in, then lowered her eyes swiftly.

To Ezra, Bruce said: "Old-timer, how are you?"

Ezra stared at him, frowning. "Well enough," came the short, none-too-friendly answer. "I would like to be able to put my finger on you."

"That should be easy," smiled Bruce. "I'm right in front of you."

"There was a night," said Ezra slowly, "when you stood up right handsome in the Carling camp against the rough ones of the Rocking A. But next I hear of your standing over Hack Asbell, a

123

gun in your hand, threatening to kill any man who touched him. A man is one thing or the other. Which are you?"

"I'm a very ordinary sort of a man, Ezra. I just try and do what I think is right. Does that make me a fool?"

The gaunt settler seemed to think that over for some time. "Maybe not a fool," he conceded finally, "but still a man who is hard to figure. Yet, I've a mind to like you for the stand you made in town. I don't like mobs. So now you can light down if you want and help Tracy Carling and me eat that pie she is setting out. For it was bake day at the Carling camp and they did not forget old Ezra."

"You offer bait no man could refuse," said Bruce, swinging down. He moved over toward the girl. "With your permission, Miss Carling."

The keen pleasure he knew at sight of her was startling. It was like a fragrance, known before and then half forgotten, that had been abruptly rediscovered, bringing with it the realization that it hadn't been really forgotten at all, but instead had been unconsciously yearned for all the time.

Looking down at her, even though her head was now in shadow, it seemed that sunlight still burned in her hair, warm and glowing, faultless in its luster. And the slender grace of her shoulders was as natural and unstudied and perfect as a reed bending before the wind.

That she was conscious of his intense approval showed in the way color spread a slow stain across her cheeks. But her words were curt.

"It's Ezra's pie. He can do what he wants with it."

It was like a bucket of ice water in the face. The warmth in Bruce's eyes faded. He turned back to his horse. "On second thought, Ezra," he said stonily, "I think I'll ride on."

"No," said Ezra. "No, you won't. You'll stay like I asked you to."

"Of course," said the girl tautly. "I shouldn't have said that. I . . . I didn't mean it. Only I don't understand . . ."

"What don't you understand?" Bruce asked.

"Why you took Hack Asbell's part?" she burst out. "Have you stopped to think what a horrible thing it was that he and his men did? To hang an old, defenseless man like Jake Hendee and then to leave a sign on him . . . on his dead body? No punishment is too great for a man who would do a thing as brutal and wicked as that!"

Her eyes weren't lowered now. They were flaming at him.

"I agree with you," Bruce told her. "No punishment is too great. Only . . . Hack Asbell and his men did not do it. That is why I took Asbell's side against the mob."

"How can you say that?" she stormed. "The sign . . . ?"

125

"Any man could have written that and pinned it on Jake Hendee's body," said Bruce quietly. "There is no proof that the Rocking A was responsible. I have Hack Asbell's word for it that his outfit had nothing to do with the Hendee affair, and he's too proud a man to lie."

"But Jason Spelle says the Rocking A is responsible. And Jason wouldn't lie, either."

"He could be mistaken."

"Maybe you're forgetting how the Rocking A riders came into our camp, ready to abuse and bully and tear things apart," Tracy Carling insisted. "Though you shouldn't, for you were the one who stopped them from doing it."

"That was foolish business on the part of Rocking A, which they now realize. There'll be no more of it."

"How do you know?"

"Because," said Bruce gravely, "I'm foreman of the outfit now."

At this she came fully to her feet. "You! Foreman of the Rocking A? So that's it! No wonder you saved Asbell's murderous old neck. No wonder you stand up for him and deny his lies. It means a job for you. And that's all that matters, isn't it?" The scorn she threw at him made him squirm inside.

He retreated far back within himself. "You're jumping at unfair conclusions," he said harshly.

She did not answer. She turned her back and

marched away, swinging along, slim and defiant, toward her uncle's camp, which lay beyond a roll of the prairie, some half mile distant. Bruce Martell watched her, his face a mask.

"Well, now," growled Ezra Banks. "I can hardly blame the lass, for I wonder myself about your being foreman of the Rocking A. A night or two ago you were no part of that outfit, so you said then. What's a man to believe?"

"That's something you'll have to figure out for yourself,"

Bruce said bitterly. "You look at a man and you make your guess. You believe him or you don't. I'm certain of only one thing right now, which is that I'm probably creation's biggest fool. I don't know why I should give a thin damn as to what goes on in this basin or to the people in it. Yet I do. For my brother Kip is here and deserves his chance. And then there are women like Aunt Lucy Carling, too good for a stupid world filled with crooked men. If you want to know more, Ezra . . . be at Pat Donovan's store at ten tonight. Thanks for the offer of the pie. Afraid I couldn't enjoy it now."

He stepped into the saddle and let the black run.

Chapter Thirteen

Besides Pat Donovan there were eleven men in the store when Bruce Martell stepped through the door of it that night, a few minutes before 10:00. One of these was Ezra Banks and with him was a solid-looking man of middle age with a good mouth and direct, grave eyes. There was a small stir at Bruce's entrance.

He looked over at Donovan and asked: "Any more due, Pat?"

"These will be all," answered the storekeeper.

Bruce turned and locked the store door. Then he strode over to the counter and turned to face the room.

"If you didn't know it before," he said quietly, "my name is Bruce Martell. I came into Indio Basin to find my younger brother. Aside from Kip I knew no one in the basin when I arrived. Things have happened since that have now made me foreman of the Rocking A. There is no use in my going further unless you men stand ready to believe what I'm going to say. How about it?"

They looked him over, stirring a little. These men, Bruce saw, meeting their grim scrutiny, were good men and solid, all of them definitely the more worthy type of settler. One of them cleared his throat: "Depends on what you're going to ask us to believe. But we're willing to listen."

Bruce nodded. "That's fair enough. Here's the first item. The Rocking A did not lynch Jake Hendee."

"What proof you got of that?" growled a settler.

"A good man's word."

"Hack Asbell's?"

"Hack Asbell's."

"Rocking A was riding pretty wild the night Hendee was lynched," said the grave-eyed man with Ezra Banks. "My name is Brink Carling. I've my wife's and my niece's word for it that they came barging into my camp and that you're the very man who cooled off the rough stuff they intended."

"That's true," Bruce agreed. "The Rocking A boys weren't using their heads then, which they now know and admit. But they all have told me flatly that they did not go near Hendee's camp. I believe them because there would be no point in their denying the Hendee business . . . if they were responsible. If they had hung Jake Hendee, and put a sign on him proclaiming the fact, why would they deny it later?"

"That makes sense," said another settler. "But if Rocking A didn't lynch Hendee, who did, and why?"

"That's the answer I'm looking for," said Bruce. "Which one of you men is Otten?"

"Here," said a short, square-jawed man. "I'm Otten."

"You knew Jake Hendee. You and others went over Hendee's camp to take care of his effects. What was it you thought should be there, but didn't find?"

"A real chunk of money," said Otten, "which Jake got for the property he sold back home before coming on this rush. I know he had a widowed sister back there and I wanted to see that she got what Jake had. We couldn't find a cent around the camp, but there was a trunk in his wagon that somebody had opened, after busting the lock. Jake should have had around fifteen thousand dollars with him."

This information brought a decided stir among those present. "What you're getting at then, Martell," said Brink Carling, "is that those who lynched Hendee also robbed him?"

"Right! And how better cover up their tracks than by putting a sign on him that would point at the Rocking A? And you must admit that Rocking A would have had not the slightest idea that Hendee had fifteen thousand dollars in his wagon, or fifteen cents."

A settler named Martin, bearded and with flaming blue eyes, said: "We're listening plenty now, Martell. Go on."

"I've seen quite a few settlers and their outfits since I hit this basin," said Bruce. "There are a lot of plenty substantial people in Indio Basin. They're not a flock of broken-down, poverty-stricken, lath-and-tar-paper shack squatters. They are men with good wagons, good equipment, with money in their pockets, come to take over a chunk of good new earth and to build substantially on it. In other words, there are a lot of Jake Hendees in the basin. And rich pickings for somebody out to kill and rob, while using the Rocking A as a handy scapegoat to point a finger at. Think over that possibility."

The rumble of voices ran over the room. Bruce built a cigarette and waited. Presently Pete Martin turned his burning eyes on Bruce. "There would have to be some kind of an organization working together and undercover to pull that sort of thing. You got any answer to that?"

"Nothing definite," Bruce told him. "I've got some ideas. I'd have to run them down before I could be sure. I'm willing to take over the chore if you men will agree to help."

"How can we help?" demanded Martin.

"By calling off the dogs where Rocking A is concerned. By doing all you can to counteract all this blind hostility toward Rocking A. Somebody in this basin has sold the settlers a bill of goods against Rocking A, and a false one. Against all men of the saddle, for that matter. The day I rode into Indio Basin I had settlers cuss me, growl at me, and finally force a fight on me. My only crime was that I was a saddle man."

"You've got to admit that Hack Asbell has given cause for being cussed," said Brink Carling. "His men haven't been exactly gentle with some of the folks."

"True enough," Bruce admitted. "But Hack's changed. He told me himself that he's got no quarrel with you settlers about this basin land. He's satisfied with the range he's got north of Hayfork River. But somebody *has* been slow-elking some of his beef, and naturally that burns him plenty. And you can't blame him for that."

"Then why don't he sell us some beef?" growled still another of the settlers. "He's got plenty of it, and we got none. A few beefsteaks under their belts would change the attitude of a lot of folks toward Asbell."

"That's going to be done," said Bruce. "Within a couple of days you'll be able to buy all the Rocking A beef you want, right over Pat Donovan's counter. You can spread the word to that effect."

Pete Martin came doggedly back to the other issue. "How do you figure to go about running down them responsible for Jake Hendee?"

"By riding, looking, listening, and reading signs," said Bruce. "I'll probably have some of the Rocking A 'punchers riding with me. But we don't want every settler we pass to be suspecting us of being out on some sort of dirty work. That's where you men come in. Talk a little tolerance among the other settlers and make them realize we're out to help their interests instead of to hurt them. Rocking A doesn't like to be accused of things they haven't done. They want to prove somebody has been lying. Rocking A knows that you settlers are in Indio Basin to stay. Rocking A intends to stay in business, too, and has sense enough to know they've got to be on terms of friendship with the basin folks to do this. There's no mystery about Rocking A's new attitude. It's plain common sense. Well?"

Pat Donovan spoke up. "I've been running this store here in Starlight long before any settler ever put foot in Indio Basin. I've known Hack Asbell for years. He's a stubborn man but a square one. His given word is beyond question. You have it now through Martell here. You'd be fools not to believe it."

"I've got one more question," said Brink Carling. "Why wasn't Jason Spelle included in this gathering? Jason is one of us and a mighty influential man across Indio Basin. He could do more to spread good will for the Rocking A than any man I know. How about that, Martell?"

Pat Donovan spoke quickly. "Suppose I answer that, Brink Carling. Nobody can accuse me of prejudice. I run my store, meet every man fair. I've got no axe to grind with anybody. But I have a mind that asks questions of itself. I ask myself just what Jason Spelle wants out of this basin? As far as I can find out, the man has staked or filed on no land. And if he doesn't want land in this basin, what does he want? I hear him constantly preaching against Hack Asbell and the Rocking A. Why? What has Hack Asbell ever done to him personally? I say this Jason Spelle is one big question mark to which I get no satisfactory answer. Bluntly put, I mistrust the man, just as I mistrust any man who would be all things to everyone else and nothing to himself. Human nature just doesn't run that way. Now can you find a better answer, Brink Carling?"

There was a long moment of taut silence. Then Pete Martin said harshly: "Damn you, Donovan . . . you've made me uneasy in my mind."

Sam Otten said: "Pat, you admit to thoughts I've had myself, but never had nerve enough to speak. Friends, it's a question we can all ponder on. Just what does Jason Spelle want in Indio Basin?"

A sound came in from the dark street, the pound of heavy hoofs, running. Pat Donovan went to the door and looked out. A heavy work horse came to a lumbering stop in front of the store. A man dropped off the animal, ran across the store porch. Donovan let him in. A settler, a waspy man, small and thin-faced. Donovan knew him and called him by name.

"Moss Riddle! What's all the hurry about, man?"

134

"Dopkins," panted Riddle. "Feller on the next quarter-section to me. Lynched! That damned Rocking A again!"

"Another . . . lynched? How do you know?"

"How do I know? God damn it, man . . . I saw him . . . hangin' to his own wagon tongue. Where's Jason Spelle? He's got to know about this."

Bruce Martell was now at Moss Riddle's side, towering over him. And when Riddle, seeing that Jason Spelle was not in the store, would have hurried out, Bruce caught him by the shoulder and pulled him back.

"Wait a minute, friend. I want to know more about this. You say you saw a man who'd been lynched. You said Rocking A did it. I want to know about that."

Moss Riddle spat at Bruce like an angry cat, tried to pull away. "You damned saddle pounders . . . damned murderin' whelps! Lynchin' decent settlers in the dark. Who in God's name do you think you are? Get your hands off me!"

But Bruce pulled Riddle deeper into the room. Over his shoulder he said bleakly: "Lock that door again, Pat. All right, friend. Now let's have the story . . . all of it."

"That's right," said Pete Martin. "Let's have it."

Riddle was quieting a little, so Bruce let go of him. The waspy settler brushed a hand across his eyes as though trying to push aside an ugly picture.

"The wife an' me had just turned in. There was a shot, over at Dopkins's camp. Right after that I heard horses runnin' like a bunch of riders was fadin' out. Rememberin' Jake Hendee, I figgered I better go have a look. The wife felt that way, too. So I did. An' there was Dopkins, like I said, hangin' to his own wagon tongue. I hotfoot back to my own camp, git up on one of my wagon team, an' come on into town. That's it. Now where . . . ?"

"Just a minute," cut in Bruce. "You said the Rocking A was there. That a guess?"

"Guess, hell!" snapped Riddle. "I know they were. There's a horse layin' there by Dopkins's camp . . . a saddled horse. Dead. It packs a Rockin' A brand. I stumbled right over it. I lit a match an' took a look. A sorrel bronc', branded Rockin' A. With the saddle still on it. And the initials H.A. stamped on the saddle cantle. H.A. . . . Hack Asbell. I figger that when they jumped him, Dopkins got off a shot an' killed Asbell's horse. Now, do you still say I'm guessin'?"

It filled the room like a dark tide, the massed and rising judgment of these settler men. Bruce Martell felt it pushing at him, measuring and weighing him. He swung a slow glance around, met the suspicion and bitter anger in their eyes.

"Something you should know," he said grimly. "A chore Hack Asbell asked me to do before I left Rocking A headquarters this evening.

I was to stop in at Joe Leggett's livery barn and pick up Asbell's horse. It's been there ever since he rode it in the day of that mob affair. When I got Asbell out of town that night, I took him on my horse. So tonight I'm to pick up his horse. A sorrel, and the gear would naturally be Asbell's own saddle. Now we hear that a horse lies dead, out at this Dopkins's camp, with the saddle still on it. A strange thing, strange enough to stand looking into. I want you men to come with me while I ask this Joe Leggett some questions."

Surprisingly it was gaunt Ezra Banks who nodded agreement to this. "A fair request," he boomed. "And makes sense."

"I'm not goin' anywhere," snapped Moss Riddle. "I want to find Jason Spelle and . . ."

"You'll come along with us," broke in Bruce. "Don't make me take you by the scruff of the neck. There's a lot riding on what this night shows. Either I've been lied to and made a fool of, or the boot is on the other foot. Gentlemen, come along."

They did, to a man, with Pat Donovan dousing the store lights, locking up, and moving out with the rest.

They found Joe Leggett already asleep on his bunk in the stable harness room. Somebody found a lantern and lit it. Joe Leggett blinked stupidly into the light.

"Hack Asbell left a horse here, along with the

saddle gear," said Bruce curtly. "Where's the bronc' and gear, Leggett?"

The stable owner mumbled under his breath, dug into a pocket of his shirt, and brought out a scrap of paper. He handed it to Bruce.

"When I come back from getting my evening grub, this was stuck in the crack of the door of this room. That's all I know."

Bruce smoothed the paper, held it close to the lantern. He read the scrawl on it aloud.

> Joe
> The boss sent me in after his sorrel bronco.
> I'm leaving this so you'll know the bronco wasn't stolen.
>
> Carp Bastion

A murmur ran through the listening settlers.

"You see!" spat Moss Riddle. "The Rockin' A was ridin' tonight an' . . ."

"Shut up!" snapped Bruce. "Joe, what time was it you went to eat?"

"Right after dark," blurted Leggett. "Getting close to seven, I guess. My usual time. I always eat a little late, what with the usual evening chores around the stable keeping me busy."

"Was Hack Asbell's horse here when you left?"

"Sure was. It was next to the last horse I grained before heading for the nose bag myself."

"Thanks, Joe," said Bruce. He turned to the

settlers. "You have Joe Leggett's word for it that Hack Asbell's horse and gear were right here in this stable between six and seven o'clock tonight. Now here is a note left for Joe when he came back to explain how the horse disappeared. It seems to have been written and signed by Carp Bastion of the Rocking A. Only there is one big thing wrong with the picture. I ate my supper in the cook shack of the Rocking A this night. That was between six and seven o'clock. And at that time Carp Bastion was sitting across the table from me. Carp is an ordinary mortal human. He couldn't have been in two places at once. What do you think, gentlemen?"

"Godfrey," muttered one of the settlers. "I don't know what to think!"

"I know what you're thinking, Martell," said Pete Martin. "You're thinking that that note is a fake. You're thinking that Asbell's horse was lifted by somebody, taken out to the Dopkins camp, shot, and left there as planted evidence against the Rocking A. Right?"

"Exactly right. Has anybody got a better guess?"

"You could be lyin'," said Moss Riddle acidly. "I don't trust no saddle pounder."

"You'll have to trust me tonight, friend," Martell told him harshly. "For I'm going out to the Dopkins camp and you're going to show me the way."

Brink Carling spoke up. "I want to see this myself. Ezra Banks and me come into town in my spring wagon. We got room for three or four more if anybody else is interested."

"I came in my own buckboard," said Pete Martin. "I can take a couple."

"Joe," said Pat Donovan, "hook a team to that three-seated carry-all of yours. I'll haul the rest of the boys."

They headed out through the wide night, three loaded wagons, and Bruce Martell in his saddle, riding beside Moss Riddle, who sat his bare-backed heavy wagon horse in an uncomfortable, hunched, and angry silence.

Cold satisfaction lay in Bruce Martell. It had cost the life of another settler, but here, thrust right into his hands, was evidence that the most doubting of the settlers in those following wagons could not ignore or misread. Those behind the dark trails being cut across the basin land had overreached this night. They had schemed deeply, but their scheming had back-fired, because they could not know that Bruce Martell had eaten supper at the Rocking A at a time to prove that the note left at Joe Leggett's door was a flat lie.

The Dopkins camp lay still and cold under the stars. They gathered in a group and looked at the figure hanging from the propped-up wagon pole. Then they cut the rope and lowered the figure to the earth. They had brought lanterns and some of them began looking over Dopkins's wagon and effects. Bruce Martell headed the group that gathered around the dead Rocking A horse. The animal had been shot through the head, almost between the eyes, in fact.

Bruce Martell let out a little exclamation, held the lantern close.

"Take a good look," he said. "The hair around that bullet hole is slightly scorched. The gun that killed this horse wasn't over two feet away when the shot was fired. Ask yourselves if Dopkins could have been that close? I don't think so. But somebody else, say a man in a saddle and leading this horse, could have been. Remember these items, gentlemen."

They went back to the wagon where Brink Carling, Sam Otten, and Pat Donovan had concluded their search, and were now kneeling beside Dopkins's body.

"We found nothing of interest in the wagon," said Donovan. "But look here."

Dopkins's shirt had been pulled out of his jeans and hung loose. Pat Donovan had pulled it up to expose the dead man's middle. Around his waist on his undershirt lay a stain of sweat and dust and a darkness that could have been oil-worked from a belt of some sort.

" 'Tis just such a mark that a money belt would leave," said Donovan slowly. "But there is no money belt now. I would say that this poor devil was robbed as well as murdered."

"Just like Jake Hendee was robbed!" burst out Sam Otten savagely. "Just like Jake Hendee was murdered."

"The evidence," said Bruce Martell, "is adding up. But there has to be more. How much more of this night can you men spare?"

"All of it," said Brink Carling, "if it'll prove who did this damnable thing."

"That will come," Bruce told him. "But first I want to prove who did not do it. Put a blanket over this unfortunate and come along."

They rode and drove the longer miles farther out from town. They crossed the river and climbed the long slope to Rocking A headquarters. Bruce went into the sleeping bunkhouse, lit a lamp, and called the settlers in. Sleep befuddled, tousled heads lifted from bunks, staring and bewildered.

"What the hell, Bruce?" stuttered Carp Bastion. "What is this, a raid?"

"No raid, Carp. Nothing to get excited about. What did you boys do after I left this evening?"

"Played poker and went to bed. Why?"

There was no guile in Carp Bastion. He was speaking the simple truth and every settler knew it.

Brink Carling said: "This is the man supposed to have written that note, Martell?"

"This is the one."

"What note?" blurted Carp. "What the devil's this all about?"

"Forget it and go back to sleep," said Brink Carling. "Sorry to have disturbed you men. I'm convinced. Rocking A had nothing to do with that deal. I'm going home. Martell, drop by my camp in the morning, will you?"

"I'll be there," agreed Martell. "I'd take you in to see Hack Asbell, only Hack ain't as young as he used to be and he got a mean knock on the head with that rock. He needs his sleep."

"I'm convinced," said Carling again. "I don't need to see anything more. Something has been accomplished this night."

The wagons rattled away. Martell put up his horse and went back to the bunkhouse, to be bombarded with a hundred questions. He told the story tersely and the import of it cooled even Carp Bastion's explosive nature.

"What's it goin' to mean?" asked Carp.

"Maybe gunsmoke along the trail," Martell told him.

Butte Allen was sharp-minded. "Riders are pulling this dirty work, Bruce. The settlers won't ever be able to run them down. Only other riders can do that. Which could mean . . . us."

"That's probably what it will amount to, Butte."

"Me," growled Carp, "even when I make a darn' fool of myself, I'm willin' to stand and

143

face judgment and take all the blame comin' my way. But when anybody pulls a crooked deal and then tries to make it look like I done it . . . that guy I want to get my hands on, even if I have to chase him across the hot hinges of hell. So, when-ever you say ride, Bruce . . . I'll be Johnny at the cookie jar."

Chapter Fourteen

Bruce Martell rode into the Carling camp a couple of hours after sunup. In the distance a buckboard was just topping a roll of prairie in the direction of town, a thin funnel of dust lifting behind it. Brink Carling was standing, sober and grave of face, staring after the vanishing rig. He turned and lifted a hand to Bruce as the black horse came to a halt.

At the fire, Tracy Carling was bending over a steaming wash boiler while, a little to one side, Aunt Lucy was up to her elbows in a galvanized washtub of snowy suds. A wash line, strung from one end of the big wagon to a post driven in the ground, was already aflutter with drying clothes.

Bruce lifted his hat to the two women, then swung down and faced Brink Carling. He jerked his head at the distant rig and said: "Early company, eh?"

Carling nodded. "Jason Spelle. The man's hard to convince."

"He knows about last night, then?"

"Yes. The word has spread. Probably Moss Riddle saw to that. Spelle said things are pretty angry in town."

"Of course he's insisting that Rocking A was responsible?" said Bruce dryly.

"That's right." Carling stared at the ground, frowning. "He insists that I and the rest were fooled last night."

"Do you think you were?"

"I know we weren't," said Carling quietly. "A man must believe the evidence of his own eyes and ears and cold judgment. But Spelle is hot-headed and hates Rocking A and everything connected with it. Frankly I don't know why he should."

"Did you tell him what you and the other settlers who were in on last night's doings have made up your minds to?"

Carling nodded. "I told him. I asked him to give us a helping hand in quieting so much of this suspicion and animosity toward Rocking A."

"And he wouldn't agree to that, of course?"

"No, he wouldn't. You seemed sure of that. Why?"

Bruce shrugged, building a smoke. "I had a real good look at him when I faced him across Hack Asbell's senseless body. There are times when, no matter how carefully a man guards against it, he lets the curtain lift a little to show what's behind it. Spelle did, at that moment."

Brink Carling stirred restlessly. "You suggest something ugly."

"What I saw wasn't pretty," said Bruce bluntly.

Aunt Lucy came over to them, drying her hands on her apron. She was smiling, but there was a

146

shadow far back in her fine eyes. "How is that wounded arm coming along, Bruce Martell?"

Bruce swung the arm in a circle. "Just like that, ma'am." He smiled back. "I bless you a dozen times a day."

She studied him intently, nodded at what she saw, then spoke gravely. "I hope I never have to doctor you for a worse hurt."

She went back to her washing. Brink Carling said: "You're going into town?"

"That's right. Aim to give Pat Donovan a hand in getting things ready to handle the beef we'll be bringing in."

"Think it's wise, with the town upset and angry?"

"Rocking A can't wait until everybody in the basin loves us. We've got things to do."

"More trouble just now won't help toward an era of good feeling," cautioned Carling.

"If trouble comes, it won't be of our making. We've got to be as aggressive about this thing as Spelle is. We can't let him do all the talking and opinion forming. Somewhere along the line the man has to be called off. Might as well be now as later."

"When I asked you to drop by this morning," said Carling, "my idea was to suggest that Rocking A keep out of sight until I and the others who were along last night had time to spread a few truths around. Frankly I intended getting hold of Jason Spelle and enlisting his help. I see now that that wouldn't have done any good. He won't listen. It leaves me up in the air."

Bruce looked at the settler gravely. Here, he realized, was a good, sound man, one whose life had been based on decent living and quiet, sane thinking. There was no violence in him at all, only a deep and abiding dislike of it. He was tolerant of other men and would not see evil in them because he did not want to see it. He was the kind who made up the sound balance in any law-abiding community. But there were many things about evil men and their ways that he did not and never would fully understand.

Bruce turned back to his horse. "Let's not fool ourselves, Mister Carling. The things that are wrong in this basin will never be corrected by soft talk. All we can do is spread as much truth as possible, and then use whatever other tools we have to get results. Those responsible for the death and robbery of Hendee and Dopkins understand only one language. I know. I've met up with their kind before. As you know by this time, the decent settlers have not a thing to fear from the Rocking A. The other kind . . ." Bruce shrugged.

He looked at Tracy Carling. She had ignored his presence completely. She continued to do so now. But what he could see of her face, as she bent over the steaming wash boiler, showed a subdued and troubled moodiness.

As the thump of the black's hoofs faded into the distance, Aunt Lucy moved over to the girl's side.

"There rides a good man, my dear. You could have given him a smile and a cheerful word. He was hoping for it. I could tell that from the way he looked at you."

The girl brushed back a wayward lock of her lovely hair with a gesture almost angry. "I still think Jason is right . . . about everything."

"I wonder," murmured Aunt Lucy, moving away. "I wonder if you really do. Blind trust and confidence are worthy, at times. They can also be stark foolishness."

Ezra Banks was not at his camp when Bruce Martell rode through. Which suited Bruce all right, for he had no wish to talk with the gaunt settler just now, nor with anyone else. He was thinking of Tracy Carling and the way she had completely ignored him. He had known real eagerness riding into the Carling camp. After last night, he had reason to expect a change in her attitude. Surely her uncle had told her the story that exonerated Rocking A. Which should have changed her mood. But it hadn't.

Just why, Bruce argued with himself, should he give a damn, anyway? What was the opinion of this settler girl to him? Women had counted for little in his life before. If he was smart, he'd keep it that way. So he told himself savagely.

And knew immediately that there was no good in trying to kid himself. Tracy Carling and her opinion did matter—mightily. It mattered more than he could put in words. He was all twisted up inside. The vision of her shining head was before him, always. It was something that had come on him gradually, but now it had him hopelessly.

That damned faker, Jason Spelle. He was the one who had filled Tracy Carling's mind with lies and suspicions. Yes, he could thank Spelle for that. Abruptly Bruce knew exactly what he was going to do. He was going to have a talk with Jason Spelle. It wouldn't be a pleasant one, but there were going to be some blue chips laid on the table. He urged the black to a faster pace.

Chapter Fifteen

A new day's business had Starlight stirring and active. This time Bruce did not ride to the back of Donovan's store and leave his horse there. That sort of thing was done with. From now on all roads and trails were his as much as any other man's, and he intended claiming his share of them. The street of Starlight was no exception. Bruce tied at the rail in front of the store.

Wagons were rolling up and down the street. Groups of settlers were gathered here and there. Bruce felt their glances and, even at a distance, the weight of their animosity. He gave them back stare for stare, then went into the store. Pat Donovan and his clerks were bustling and busy, but on catching Bruce's eye, Donovan jerked his head toward his office and, after Bruce made his way there, soon joined him.

"That fool Spelle," said Donovan bluntly. "He's at it with every bit of smooth gab he can rake up. The word is out, of course, about Dopkins, and Spelle is making the most of it. Sam Otten and Pete Martin and Ezra Banks are out about town somewhere, doing what they can to switch the tide of talk, but I've no idea what luck they're having. I had a session with Spelle myself this morning, telling him to be careful of making talk which last night proved to be a lie.

He laughed in my face. Bruce, the man is a rascal . . . and dangerous."

Bruce nodded. "I'm having a talk with him myself, with the gloves off. I didn't want to get rough before, Pat. My first chore was to clear Rocking A in the eyes of at least a few sound men. Now that I've done that, I can begin putting the pressure on. Yeah, I'm going looking for Spelle."

He went out into the street again and along the street. He saw Spelle's buckboard tied in front of the Land Office, so he turned in there. Cashel Edmunds was busy with a couple of late filers, but soon they went out. Edmunds looked at Bruce stonily.

"Where's Spelle?" rapped Bruce.

Edmunds shrugged. "I wouldn't know."

"I think you do. His buckboard is out front. Where is he?"

Edmunds slapped his counter with an angry hand. "Listen, Martell. In this office . . ."

"No, you listen, Edmunds. In this office or anywhere else, you rate damned small with me. I saw you tip off that settler to throw the rock that downed Hack Asbell. A coward's trick. Don't try and stand tall and straight in front of me. You tipped your hand then. So come down off your high horse. Where's Spelle?"

Cashel Edmunds tried to hold the impact of Bruce's hard stare. He wasn't up to it. He licked his lips and looked away.

"In The Frontier, I think," he muttered sulkily. "I'm not his keeper."

Bruce turned, started to leave, then paused. Jason Spelle had just stepped out of The Frontier and was headed for the Land Office. Bruce moved back from the door, waited. Spelle was speaking harshly even as he came to the threshold.

"Listen, Cash. I want you to get hold of . . . !"

Spelle broke off with a start, squaring swiftly around to face Bruce fully. Bruce grinned mirthlessly.

"You sure take in a lot of space, Spelle. The way you give orders! I thought Edmunds was running this Land Office. Could I have been mistaken?"

Spelle's pale brown eyes, widening in his first surprise, now pulled to a narrowed guardedness. "What do you want?" he rapped thinly.

"What makes you think I want anything?" Bruce retorted. "Something worrying you?"

"You got a hell of a nerve," charged Spelle. "After last night. I understand you're now the foreman of Rocking A. Pretty smooth, what you pulled last night. Holding a little get-together in Donovan's store . . . putting on a great show of righteousness, while all the time the rest of your damned crew were out murdering that poor devil, Dopkins. You might have fooled some gullible ones, Martell. But you're not fooling me."

"That," said Bruce, "is something I can hand right back to you, Spelle. You're fooling a lot of people, but not me. And not several other good men who are beginning to get their eyes open. Matter of fact, I did want something when I came in here. I wanted to see you, so that I could tell you a few things, right in your teeth. First is . . . that you're a damned, loose-mouthed liar. Do I make that plain? A lousy, snake-in-the-weeds liar. And I hope you try and make something of it."

For a brief moment, Bruce thought Spelle would try. He saw the blaze build in the man's eyes, a blaze that seemed to turn them from brown to a moiling yellow, wild and raging. He saw the ripple of fury run up Spelle, clear from his heels, and he saw Spelle's taut features pull into a beaked, thin-lipped mask. But it went no further.

"I don't take the bait, Martell," burst out Spelle hoarsely. "You're a gunfighter . . . just a cheap killer. Even if I carried a gun, which I don't, I wouldn't be fool enough to let you badger me into going for it, so you'd have an excuse to shoot me down."

Bruce's laugh was taunting. "Now you're lying again. Why do you always wear a coat, Spelle, in weather that puts other men in their shirt sleeves? I'll tell you why. Because you do pack a gun, and you got one on now . . . in a shoulder holster. Let's see you take your coat off and prove me wrong. If I am, I'll back out of here on my hands and knees and you can kick me in the teeth all the way."

Jason Spelle fairly trembled with the rage that gripped him.

Bruce laughed again. "You see, I'm right. Once a liar, always a liar. So that's one thing I wanted to tell you. Here's something else. You've made it a business to spread a lot of poison talk against the Rocking A, an outfit that has never harmed you personally in any way. Now I'm warning you to lay off. Anything that is truth, Rocking A doesn't mind being said about it. But your kind of lies is something else again. You spill any more of them and we make you hard to catch. That's cold crow, Spelle. Chew on it."

Bruce waited for Spelle to answer. He'd been rough in this thing, deliberately so and for many reasons. Not the least of these was because of a fair-haired settler girl who had, this very morning, refused to consider that Bruce Martell even existed. And, Bruce told himself savagely, this was something he could thank Jason Spelle for.

Spelle held on to himself. He made no answer. He just stood there, hating Martell venomously. Which told something no sane man could overlook. The fact that Spelle had refused to allow himself to be taunted into a violent move proved the dangerous potential of the man. Spelle might be a liar, but he was no fool.

Bruce backed to the door, paused there a moment. "You know, Spelle," he said, "I'm a great believer in the idea that what every man does, he does for a purpose. I just can't believe that your apparent fond concern for every settler in this basin springs from the fact that you're just overflowing with the milk of human kindness. I'm convinced that you want and expect something out of this deal. It'll be interesting to find out just what that something is. I expect to find out."

Bruce moved on through the door, stood watching it from outside for a moment, then started down the street.

In the Land Office, Jason Spelle began to curse, in a low, strangled voice. The bottled-up rage in the man came out of him in an ugly tide. It poured across his writhing lips, it came out of his pores in sliming sweat, and it shook him physically like some bitter ague.

Cashel Edmunds watched Spelle, mixed emotions mirrored on his face. There was some awe, some contempt, some fear. "That's doing no good," he said. "Martell can't hear you. If he could, you wouldn't be saying it."

Spelle whirled on him and for a moment Edmunds thought the man would come clawing at his throat. He backed away, got the counter between him and Spelle.

"You should talk!" raged Spelle. "Don't forget, my friend, you're in this as deep as I am. If I go down, you go down. As for Martell, he'll be dead inside the next half hour. That's all provided for. And I can wait that long to laugh!"

Chapter Sixteen

Bruce Martell went back to Donovan's store, and at sight of him the storekeeper let out a sigh of relief. "You didn't find him?"

"I found him. I lathered him pretty heavy. He didn't rise to the bait. The man's smart enough to be dangerous, Pat."

"He's dangerous, all right," agreed Donovan. "Any man who can sway a lot of fools and never loses a chance to do it is always dangerous."

Donovan had a broad sheet of paper spread on one end of his counter and was laboriously lettering a rough sign. It read:

> Starting tomorrow fresh beef will be for sale in this store. Prices fair and quality guaranteed.

He chewed his tongue as he finished it, and then grinned at Martell. "Want to add anything?"

Martell shook his head. "That says everything."

Hammers were clattering and saws whining out back of the store. Here, in one corner of the big storeroom, a smaller, double-walled room was rapidly taking shape. Four men were working furiously.

"Had 'em at it ever since you first offered the

beef deal," said Donovan. "It won't be perfect, but it'll do for the time being. I don't expect to have to hold any of that beef very long."

They went outside and put up the sign, Martell holding it in place while Donovan drove tacks. A passing settler stared and spelled out the words with moving lips.

"That mean what it says, Donovan?"

"I ain't putting the sign up just to decorate the store," Donovan told him.

"Where you gettin' that fresh beef?"

"Rocking A. Legitimate beef, too. No slow-elked stuff. Spread the word, friend . . . there'll be plenty for everybody."

"Rockin' A, huh? Well, now . . . that's somethin' I never expected to see. I'll tell the missus. She's been wantin' some."

The settler went his way. Martell drawled: "You see, Pat? By the time that *hombre* gets through talking it over with his wife, neither of 'em will be nearly as mad at Rocking A as they were."

Bruce started back into the store. Pat, following, glanced along and across the street, thinking that, given time, Starlight would be five times the town it now was, thriving and substantial. And any man who, like one Pat Donovan, had his business roots well set and deep would be fixed for life. It was a good future.

And then all of the genial Irishman's thoughts seemed to freeze into a solid ball inside his head, for, as his glance came back and ran the length of his store porch, he saw there, at the far corner of the building, a leveled gun. Behind the gun was the arm and shoulder of a man, and behind these the man's face. A narrow, malevolent face, still showing the effects of violent contact with a beer bottle. Bully Thorpe's face.

At the same moment, across the street, some twenty yards between them, two other lank, gangling figures moved into view. One held a ready rifle in his hands, half raised. The other two Thorpes, Dyke and Whip. Pat Donovan did not see these two, which was perhaps as well. Else his voice would certainly have strangled in his throat. As it was, he managed a sharp, breaking cry.

"Martell! Look out . . . !"

When a man had walked much with danger, particularly the kind of danger Bruce Martell had known in the days when he had marshaled towns like Rawhide and Ravensdale, he had reactions to it that were instinctive and flashing fast, both mental and physical. Either he had these, or he did not live long. And Bruce Martell had lived.

A man of slower mind and body, less critically trained, might have paused in some wonderment at Pat Donovan's warning, and so died, then and there. But with Martell the words were hardly past Donovan's lips before he was into the store doorway in an explosive, spinning leap. And by so doing avoided the slug that came within inches of taking the whole back of his head off, before gouging a long furrow along the face of the store and showering Pat Donovan with stinging splinters. The hoarse rumble of the gun hit the street like a thunderclap.

Pat Donovan was no coward. Neither was he a fool. He knew when discretion was the better part of valor. This exposed porch was no place for him with no weapon in his hand other than a tack hammer. It was farther to the door than it was to the safe end of the porch. So Pat went the way of the porch in a scuttling, scrambling dive, and landed on his hands and knees on the solid earth beyond.

As Bruce Martell flashed to the temporary safety of the store door, he had his gun out, and now he whirled to jam his left shoulder against the shelter of the doorpost, his glance raking the street. He had placed the sound of that first shot, but he couldn't ignore those two gangling figures across the street, especially the one with the leveled rifle.

The rifle leaped in recoil, snarling. The doorpost shivered under the impact of the bullet and splinters flew. Something tugged sharply at Martell's hat. The man behind the rifle came two steps forward, levering in another cartridge.

Martell dropped his gun in line, knowing that

the wide width of the street made it a long shot for a belt gun, unless a man took the time to judge his sights and distance carefully. Again Martell's training stood him in good stead. He took that time, even though Dyke Thorpe's rifle was settling into line again.

Martell's gun bounced, jammed its recoil back against the heel of his hand, and filled the store with the pound of its report. Over there across the street speeding lead told with an ominous thud. It lifted Dyke Thorpe up on his toes, seemed to hold him there while he swayed from side to side, then fell in a slow, loose turn, his rifle crashing in report again, its bullet blowing a burst of street dust into the air.

Whip Thorpe started toward his stricken brother, changed his mind swiftly when a haze of splinters lifted from the hitch rail beside him and a slug buzzed away in droning ricochet. Whip looked for shelter and raced for it, diving past the corner of a building just ahead of another searching bullet.

Martell heard Bully Thorpe yell. "Dyke! Dyke! Whip . . . damn your yellow soul . . . !"

Martell made a guess and took his chance. He drove through the store doorway, out onto the open porch, swung low, and crouched to face the treacherous corner where Bully Thorpe waited. The guess was good, the chance legitimate.

For Bully had committed that cardinal mistake

of a gunfighter. He had let the fine focus of his attention be diverted. Seeing Dyke go down had shocked and rattled him, pulled him a couple of strides beyond the protective corner of the store building. He was staring at Dyke and cursing Whip when Bruce Martell exploded into view.

In the split second Bully Thorpe realized his mistake and tried to rectify it, tried desperately. His lips peeled back as he lunged for shelter again, trying to throw a shot at the same time. He was slow both ways. Martell's lead took him heart high, spinning him against the corner he wanted so frantically to reach. He bounced off and crumpled down.

Bruce Martell went across the street at a run, plugging fresh loads into his reeking gun. He was after Whip Thorpe, bleak and merciless. The Thorpes had started this, just as they had started that other ruckus. Now he'd finish it.

Men, crowding into the street, drawn by the roar of gunfire, stopped in their tracks and stood motionlessly, watching Martell. There was that about him that even the most dull-witted could understand and want none of. Bruce raced past the corner beyond which Whip Thorpe had dodged, went on looking for his man.

Out there at the far edge of town was a broken-down wreck of a wagon. Whip dodged behind this, pausing momentarily to look back. And when he saw Bruce Martell move into sight, he turned and ran again. For Whip knew now that both Dyke and Bully were dead, else this tall deadly figure would not be coming after him. Stark terror caught up Whip. He ran blindly. But he ran. And Martell let him go.

Martell came back to the street. The crowd was mostly in front of Donovan's store or at the corner of it. Pat Donovan was in the middle of things, bristling. The knees of Pat's pants were split and the palms of his hands skinned from violent contact with the ground, but there was nothing wrong with his spirit.

"They asked for this, the Thorpes did!" he yelled. "They started it. They were out to get Martell. They damned near got me. I tell you they started all of it!"

Sam Otten and Pete Martin were also part of the crowd. Now it was Martin, with his flaming eyes, who had his say.

"This is the kind of end that was in the cards for the Thorpes. All the way in along the road to War Lance Creek, and along the creek and after the jump-off, the story was always the same. Whenever or wherever you heard the word trouble mentioned, then you heard the name of Thorpe spoken, too. I say there was no good in any of them and never could be."

At the edge of the crowd a sullen voice said: "They were settlers and a cowman killed them. That's enough for me."

The speaker was a burly, bullet-headed man, hatless, with a thick mop of tightly curled black hair. His eyes were little, black, and flatly hard.

Another voice said: "Curly Garms said something, there."

Sam Otten spoke up sharply. "That's stupid talk. Settlers or not, the Thorpes were no damned good. Every decent person in Indio Basin that ever had any dealings with them will tell you that. They started this thing, and whether the man who took care of them sits a saddle or a wagon box makes no difference. For every man has a right to protect his own skin."

Curly Garms turned his flat, hard eyes on Otten. "There's only two sides to this argument. Settlers or cowmen. You're either for one or the other. You can't play it mealy-mouthed and try and straddle the fence."

"That's where you're wrong," retorted Sam Otten stoutly. "The two sides are right and wrong. Personally I'm getting damn' well fed up with all this blind hurrah and drum beating against the cow interests. So are a lot of other responsible settlers. We're beginning to wonder just what's behind it all. We're wondering just why Jason Spelle is carrying the torch against the cow interests. So far as I know, they've never done him any personal wrong. Now I'm wondering about you, Garms."

"How about Jake Hendee and Enos Dopkins?"

blurted Garms. "Cow interests lynched them."

"How do you know?" snapped Otten. "Did you see them? Did Spelle see them? Did anybody else see them? No . . . no all the way! In my mind and in the mind of plenty of others, the Rocking A stands completely cleared of that dirty business. I'm no damned sheep, to be led around by the nose by a tub-thumper like Jason Spelle. Time some of the rest of you opened your eyes and your minds."

Bruce Martell stood quietly, listening to this crowd wrangle. The dark mood of the moment was still on him and he turned a look on Curly Garms that made Garms shift uneasily and quiet his hostility to an unintelligible muttering. Bruce swung his glance around at the others.

"If there's any man here," he said harshly, "who's been actually harmed in any way by the Rocking A, and can step up here and prove his claim, I'll see that it's made good to him in hard money. But if you haven't been harmed, what are you hollering about?"

No one stepped up, but one man did say: "Neighbor of mine had his camp gone through by Rocking A 'punchers. They searched his wagon. Said they were looking for slow-elked beef. What d'you say to that, mister?"

"I'm not denying that it probably happened," Bruce answered. "It wasn't good headwork on the part of the Rocking A, but I can understand why they did it. Somebody's been slow-elking Rocking A beef. I know that to be a fact. Would you expect Rocking A to sit by quietly and do nothing about that sort of thing?"

"What's a few head of cows to Hack Asbell?" blurted the man. "He's got lots of them."

Bruce elbowed his way over to the fellow. "You've staked your quarter-section . . . filed on it?"

"Sure have and it's a good one."

"How about me moving in on about twenty acres of your land? You've got lots of it."

A rumble of grim amusement ran through the crowd. "I guess that answers you, Pittman," said Pete Martin.

Pittman reddened, but was argumentative. "A man's got a right to believe only what he sees. And I never saw no slow-elked beef. So, mebbe they were and mebbe they weren't."

A hand plucked at Bruce Martell's sleeve. It was Joe Leggett, the livery barn owner.

"Something mebbe you'd like to see," he mumbled. "The Thorpes' wagon. It's out back of my place. Plenty of green flies buzzin' around it."

Bruce got the implication instantly. "Everybody," he told the crowd. "Let's take a look at this."

All but one or two followed him, with Joe Leggett leading the way. The wagon was an old Conestoga, canvas ragged and patched and stained. Leggett was right about the flies. Their humming set up a thin, persistent dissonance. Inside the wagon were several sheets of tumbled canvas. These, dragged out into full sun glare, showed unmistakable stains.

Freshly butchered meat had lain on these tarps, been covered by them.

Bruce Martell's glance sought out Pittman among the crowding settlers. "I won't say a word of what I think. You give me your answer."

Stubborn as he was, Pittman had to admit the evidence. "You win, cowboy. Slaughtered beef's been hauled in this wagon, and the Thorpes never owned a beef critter in their lives. So it must have been somebody else's. I reckon you collected two of your slow-elkers this day."

In the back room of the Land Office, Jason Spelle sat with a whiskey bottle at his elbow. His face was flushed, partly with liquor, partly from the frustrated fury that still boiled in him. The beaked, predatory cast to his features was pronounced. Cashel Edmunds came into the room. Edmunds was nervous, restless. Edmunds had just returned from a trip up and down the street.

"Well?" snarled Spelle.

"They're getting away from you, Jason," said Edmunds. "This sort of thing keeps on, you won't have a dozen of those damned sod-busters willing to follow you. Those fool Thorpes!

167

Bunglers . . . bunglers all the way. They even left their wagon with a lot of blood-stained tarps where it could be found."

"Damn the wagon!" burst out Spelle furiously. "Who'd worry about the wagon if they'd just made good on the other deal? They had him dead to rights . . . dead to rights, I say. And they missed him. Bully missed him at fifty feet. And Dyke . . . standing out there . . . just because he had a rifle. That Martell . . . he's got the luck of the devil with him."

"Maybe luck . . . maybe something else," said Edmunds. "I'm remembering what Brazos said about him. Deadly."

Spelle gulped another drink. He said something that he'd said before in this same room. "He's just one man. He's mortal."

"He's still alive, and Bully and Dyke Thorpe are dead," persisted Edmunds. "And nobody could ever have a better chance than they did. Our luck began to go sour the day he rode into this basin, Jason. I don't know. I think we'd be wise to slow up."

"Slow up? Not me." Spelle emphasized this with a clenched fist banging the table beside him.

"But I tell you the settlers are slipping away from us. Martell may be lucky. But he's still deadly . . . and he's smart. He's got some damned influential men in this basin already on his side.

He's making friends and we're losing them. I don't know how he got Asbell to agree to it, but having Donovan selling fresh beef, Rocking A beef, ain't going to hurt his case at all. Give him time he'll have the settlers setting up law and order across Indio Basin . . . and he'll probably be the law."

Spelle grinned wolfishly and without mirth. "He won't have time . . . and it's a big basin. To hell with the sod-busters. They're just sheep, anyhow. All of them. I'll spread so much hell across this basin they'll be afraid to stick their heads above ground. If they're not for me, then they're against me, and will have to take the consequences."

"But I thought we needed them with us . . . on our side."

"I thought so, too. But I see now that the idea was wrong. Didn't I just say they were sheep? Well, sheep can be managed up to a point. But they stampede . . . go every which way when something unexpected jumps up. To do what we intend to do, we've got to have a bunch of men who don't scatter, or stampede . . . who don't pull and haul and stop to argue."

"Where'll we get 'em? That's the big question."

"We got Pitch Horgan and his crowd. There's more like 'em to be had. I'll get 'em. I'll be pulling out tonight. May be gone for two or three weeks. Keep your mouth shut, your eyes and ears open. Be a good idea, maybe, to let things quiet down. But when I get back, look out."

"You'll be missed," said Edmunds nervously. "People will ask questions. What'll I tell 'em?"

"Tell 'em nothing. Tell 'em you don't know where I am. Do 'em good to wonder. Only they won't, much after a day or two. They're happier with their damn' dumb noses in a plow furrow. They'll know when I get back . . . don't worry about that."

Cashel Edmunds's uneasiness grew. This was a different Jason Spelle than he had known before. There was a wildness about the man, as though something that he had kept carefully under a leash before was now free and rampant—the look of a man prepared to burn every bridge behind him, to throw everything into the pot with the sky the limit.

Cashel Edmunds was as crooked as a snake in a wagon track, but he was a sly and cautious man and, though inevitably drawn to others of his kind, preferred to lurk always in the background, to move deviously, and let scheming carry more of a load than open violence. At first he thought that in Jason Spelle he'd found a man to fit his own mold. Now he realized differently. Spelle would allow scheming as long as it worked. When it no longer did, he would go to the other extreme. And a man like that could be highly dangerous, not only to those who opposed him, but to those who worked with him; he could drag down the temple and crush not only himself, but everyone in it.

"Sod-busters may be sheep," said Edmunds, "but there are an awful lot of them, with sharp hoofs. Caught in front of enough of them a man could be cut to pieces. I wouldn't go too wild, Spelle."

Spelle looked at him with open contempt. "No, *you* wouldn't, Cash. We're both crooks, you and me. But you're just a flea-bite crook. A few dollars here, a few dollars there suits you fine. Just your meat. What do you expect to get that way?"

"I expect to keep my hide in one piece and my neck the same length it is now," answered Edmunds sulkily. "Flatly I don't like the things you're hinting at. If you go trying to run completely wild, you can count me out. I'm remembering Bully and Dyke Thorpe laying in the street. I don't like contemplating a picture of myself in the same place."

"This fellow, Martell, got you scared that bad, has he?"

"Yes," admitted Edmunds, "he has. Before he showed up, everything was working fine, just the way we figured it would. We had all the settlers with us. We had them looking the direction we wanted them to look. Hack Asbell and his outfit were just bull-headed enough to keep on playing right into our hands. In a few months we could have cleaned up . . . big. But not now. Things have changed, Jason, and the smart thing is to recognize that fact and act accordingly."

"Which," sneered Spelle, "in your case would be to lay down and quit, is that it?"

Edmunds flushed. "Maybe not quit, exactly, but at least to do some long-headed thinking."

Spelle poured himself another drink. "I've done my thinking," he said harshly. "The money that was in the settler camps before is still there. Rocking A is still there. I want all of it. I'm going after it. And you don't sneak out of the picture just because the going may be a little rough. The day you try that, Cash . . . then you'll be on the street, just like Bully and Dyke Thorpe were. And I'm the man who'll put you there. That's a promise."

Chapter Seventeen

Over settler fires across Indio Basin, in pot and pan and Dutch oven, fresh beef boiled and fried and baked. Hours before daylight every morning, a wagon loaded with beef slaughtered the late afternoon before, and cooled out during the night, rolled away from Rocking A range, jounced across the Button Willow ford of the Hayfork River and covered the miles to Starlight, there to hang in Pat Donovan's cool room. And back at Rocking A headquarters, Hack Asbell, up and around again now, looked at the money Bruce Martell placed in his hand and swore in amazement.

"Never made a better profit on a beef critter in my life," he admitted. "Or done it easier. This keeps up, I won't have to move a shipping herd across the Lodestones, son."

"It'll keep up," Bruce told him. "Pat says he can use an extra carcass tomorrow. We're selling more than beef, Hack. We're selling good will all across the basin. And I think it's about time you did a little riding around down there, dropping in on different settler camps, saying hello and getting acquainted. Those people are going to be your neighbors for a long time. There's still a few die-hards amongst them, but mostly you won't have any rocks thrown your way again."

"Huh!" grunted Asbell. "No sod-buster would ever cotton to me, or me to them. We jest ain't the same kind of folks, that's all. I'm better off sticking to my own wickiup."

Bruce showed his slow-breaking smile. "Don't be so cussed crusty. Get that chip off your shoulder. Go down there prepared to meet men with two arms and two legs just like you've got, men who happen to feel more at home at a plow handle than in the saddle, men who ask only a decent living out of the world, the same as you do. Make some friends. The day may come when you'll need 'em."

Asbell looked at Bruce narrowly. "Why do you keep saying that? You admit yourself that big-mouthed blatherskite of a Spelle seems to have drifted out. When you cleaned that Thorpe gang, you put a stop to the slow-elking. Everything's quiet. No more of that night riding an' lynching going on. Everything smooth as a fresh-licked calf."

"Right now, yes," admitted Bruce. "It won't stay that way. There's something phony in the way Spelle dropped from sight. I'm remembering the Horgan gang was around once. Maybe they still are. When things quiet down so sudden after stormy doings . . . that's the time to look out. This basin is still a long ways away from lasting peace and quiet. You do some of that riding. It'll pay off."

The grizzled cattleman scowled. "You keep on making up my mind for me and I'll end up without any. But you been right in so many other things, I got to admit you *may* be right in this. I'll do my best not to walk around them sod-busters like a stiff-legged dog around a porcupine. But I ain't promising a thing. Understand, not a thing."

Bruce watched Hack Asbell ride off, then turned back to work. There was plenty to do, what with slaughtering beef and moving it into town on schedule. This, along with the regular ranch work, kept everybody on the jump. Through Pat Donovan, Bruce had sent outside for a couple of men trained in the trade of slaughtering and handling meat. When these men arrived, things would be better, but for the present there was no idle time for anyone.

In a way, Bruce was happier than he'd been for a long time. Looking back at the tough days he'd known in Rawhide and Ravensdale, he saw that while they had been a living and a good one, yet a man paid an inevitable price at that game, even though it left him unscarred physically. For it was a game that built a shell of solitariness about a man and left him lonely. It turned him in upon himself, turned others away from him. The high wine of excitement and danger was inevitably followed by the dark moods of let-down. And out of each successive one of these a man emerged with an added burden of bleakness and grim visions of the future. A man forgot how to laugh, how to relax. He aged, while his years were still young. He might gain stature of a kind, but this very stature squeezed certain human qualities out of him that no man could afford to lose. It had been a trail no man could travel too long without finding it was too late to turn back. Bruce's hope was that he had stopped in time.

It was good to ride this foothill range, under the towering shoulders of the Lodestones. It was good to move among cattle, to read their worth and know the need of the world for them. It was good to face a chore that did not mean throwing the weight of his personality and reputation against surly, hating men. Yes, it was good to work cattle, to know the smell of them and of dust and of sweat salting up the hide of the horse under him, and to feel his own sweat working down his muscles, oiling them and making them supple.

It was especially good to come in at night, hungry and weary, to sit at the cook shack table with his crew, swap talk with them of the day's affairs, to know that he was one of them and that they liked and respected him for himself. And then to dawdle an hour or two in the bunkhouse before turning in for the night. And then, in the soft dark, to think and dream a little.

One thought always came, which was half pleasure and half a strange, irking pain. It was of Tracy Carling. He had not been near the Carling camp, since that morning when Tracy Carling had ignored him so completely. A dozen times since, when on his way to or from town, he had been mightily tempted to turn off the trail and seek the Carling camp. Each time he had resisted the impulse. He wondered if this were pride, or just plain damned stubbornness. Man, he concluded, was a queer brute, and lucky to get along through life as well as he did.

Several times he had dropped by at the Clebourne camp for an hour or two with Kip and Cadence and her father. Kip and Clebourne were already well along with the construction of a sizable cabin. It was, Kip declared, just a starter, enough to get them through the approaching winter. Next spring it would be added to, made into a real ranch home.

On these visits Bruce studied his younger brother, afraid he might discover some sign of the return of the restlessness that had given him cause for worry over the kid's future in the past. He found none. Kip's feet were on solid earth at last and would stay there.

Hack Asbell returned from his ride across the basin just before dark. Bruce, watching for him, met him at the corrals. "You look," he observed, "in as good health as when you left."

"What did you expect," growled Asbell crustily, "that I'd be all clawed and beat up?"

Bruce grinned in the dusk and ignored this. "Meet some good people?"

"Nobody kissed me on both cheeks," grumbled Asbell. "But at least they didn't sick no dogs on me. Gimme time and mebbe I can get used to some of them. Talked to one family who asked about you . . . that is, some of the family did. Folks by the name of Carling. Seems like you did 'em the favor of cooling off Carp and the boys one evening when they were riding and not using the best of judgment. There was a woman there with the nicest eyes I ever saw in a human being."

"Missus Carling, of course," murmured Bruce. "One lovely lady."

"There"—Asbell nodded—"I agree with you. There was a young 'un there, too. Girl with the prettiest hair! Reminded me of . . . well, now . . ."

"The color of aspen leaves after the first frost," suggested Bruce gravely.

"Hah!" snorted the cattleman, flashing a shrewd look at Bruce. "Darned if that ain't it, exactly. Wish't I'd had me a daughter like that. I've been looking at cows and plug-ugly 'punchers and at myself in a shaving mirror so long, is it any wonder I'm ornery as a egg-sucking 'coon? But if I'd had me a daughter like that yaller-headed girl, why then I might've put in my years living in a real ranch house instead of a danged two-three-roomed boar's nest. Son, don't you ever make the mistake I did."

"What's that, Hack?"

"Why, figuring you're big and chesty enough to travel the trail by yourself. You may figure you've got some place. But comes a day when you sorta cast up accounts and then you realize all of a sudden that you ain't got no place at all. What's that young 'un miffed at you about?"

"Is she?"

"You know danged well she is."

"I doubt she's interested enough to give a hoot one way or the other."

"That's what you think. She didn't ask about you, but I noticed that she sure listened close for my answer when the older folks did." With that, Hack Asbell stamped away.

Chapter Eighteen

The breath of fall was in the air. The nights had a bite to them, days bright but crisp. A certain mistiness lay over the world at morning and evening, bringing its own colors to fit the hour. At times gray, again purple, and by evening especially a sad and haunting violet or mysteriously luring powder blue.

A new vigor breathed from the earth. Not the warm, growing vigor of spring, but a certain lustiness, a marshaling of strength to meet the onslaughts of the coming winter. Far up in the Lodestones, bands and splotches of autumn brilliance stood out against the dark and eternal green of the conifers; a full moon rode in the night sky in solitary golden glory.

Across the miles of Indio Basin settler camps became marked with more than just a gaunt wagon or two. Cabins began shouldering up. Many of these were temporary lath-and-tar-paper shanties, but in other camps, where men had thought and prepared ahead, more substantial structures rose.

One of these was growing at the Carling camp, where Brink Carling labored with hammer and saw, with Ezra Banks helping. Ezra had already put up a one-room place at his own camp, enough for his solitary needs.

Brink Carling broke off in his work long enough to help Tracy Carling hitch the heavy work team to the big wagon. He gave Tracy a lumber list.

"Tom Nixon's men will load this for you at the lumberyard," he said.

Tracy climbed lithely to the wagon box, gathered up the reins, waved to her aunt, and sent the big wagon creaking away. She wore a trim leather jacket, buttoned to the throat against the morning's crispness, but her head was bare and the sunlight put a glow about it. Ezra Banks stared at her in frowning reflection.

"She looks like laughter and bird song," he boomed softly. "But the lass is troubled in her mind about something. What would it be, Brink?"

"I've wondered that myself," answered Carling.

"I hope it's no yearning for that Jason Spelle," growled Ezra. "For I've come to see the man as a rascal. Had he any worthwhile business in this basin, then he would not have dropped from sight the way he has. And I would like to see Bruce Martell around more than he's been."

"That Thorpe business was pretty rough," said Carling. "I watched Tracy when the word came in. She went pretty grave. That sort of thing is hard for a girl like her to understand. She's a gentle youngster."

"All of that," agreed Ezra Banks. "But life, especially in a new land like this, is not always gentle. Tracy must come to understand that. What else could Martell have done than what he did do? The Thorpes started it, and they'd have done for him if he hadn't done for them."

"I understand that," Carling said. "But I don't know that Tracy does. As for Spelle, I agree with you. I will not make the man welcome in this camp again, should he ever come back."

Riding down the slow miles to town, Tracy had her own thoughts. They were interrupted when, where the Rocking A trail cut in to join with the one she was on, a big black horse came jogging, its rider grave and tall in the saddle.

It was the first time she had seen Bruce Martell in weeks and weeks and slow color ran across her face when he looked up at her and lifted his hat. The black's swinging jog would have carried it quickly by the plodding wagon, but Martell pulled the animal down to a walk.

"There's a rope trailing behind your wagon," he called up to her. "Pull in while I gather it up for you."

Tracy obediently reined in. Martell swung the black to the rear of the wagon, was busy there a moment. Then he came clambering up along the bed of the wagon and swung himself into place beside her. She looked at him accusingly.

"There wasn't any rope trailing. You just said there was so you could tie your horse at lead and get up here on this seat."

"That's right," he admitted cheerfully. "I lied like a trooper. But it worked."

He was freshly shaven, the line of his jaw clean and darkly bronze. It was a face much more mobile than when she had seen it last. The settled, almost bitter sternness that had been so characteristic of him was not nearly so much in evidence. He looked younger, more boyish, more carefree.

"I think," he said abruptly, "that you knew darned well there was no rope trailing from this wagon. Yet you stopped."

Color touched her checks again. "That is quite true," she said. "I've been wanting to talk to you."

"Swell," he enthused. "Start in. I'm yearning to listen."

"I was wrong about something. Believing what I did of the Rocking A, I mean. I'm quite sure now that Rocking A had nothing to do with the Hendee and Dopkins affairs. So, I'm sorry for the way I acted that day at Ezra Banks's camp. You'll accept my apology?"

"Gone and forgotten. You never had cause to be sorry, anyhow. You couldn't be blamed for being mixed up. A lot of people were. How did you like my boss, Hack Asbell?"

She smiled. "I did. He tried to act such a crusty old scoundrel, but I saw right through him and he knew I did. Yes, I liked him."

"An opinion returned, with interest. He asked

me what color I thought your hair was. We finally agreed that it was aspen leaves, after the first frost. No other gold like it in all the world."

She looked away. "You're a much happier man than when I first met you. There was a grayness in you then that isn't there anymore. Hack Asbell and his Rocking A must be good for you."

"They are." Grave thoughtfulness stilled his features. "And you're right. I'm happier than ever before in my life. The old trail was a very lonely one. I never truly realized how lonely until I got off it."

"What made it so lonely?"

Bruce built a cigarette while he considered this. "The man behind a badge stands alone. Not willingly, but by necessity. On one side of the trail are those who hate him for what he is. They aren't good people, or they wouldn't hate him and . . . maybe their hate shouldn't count. Yet, it does. It's a friction that puts callouses on a man. On the other side of the trail are the better people, who, though they may respect that man behind the badge, yet they walk around him. And so the man draws in upon himself, and is lonely."

"Why did you carry the badge, knowing this?"

"I didn't know it until I'd started. Then I was too proud to quit. Besides, there is always someone who has to pack that badge. It's a job that some-one has to do, man being the strange beast he is. It would all be much simpler if each man would be a stern authority over his own conduct. This being a state of affairs the world has never seen, and never will, there will always be badges and men who must wear them."

"Would you go back to the same chore?"

"Never!" The word fairly exploded from him. "I've served my time, done my stint. I want nothing better than what I have now. A good man to work for, good comrades to ride with, and good work to find comfort in."

"Where you carried the badge . . . they were rough times and places?"

He nodded. "Rough."

"And times when you . . . you had to use that gun you carry?"

"Yes. There were others besides Bully and Dyke Thorpe. Such things happen. A man can only play the cards dealt him. That doesn't always mean he's proud of the hand he holds. Didn't I say men were strange brutes?"

A harshness had crept into his tone, some of the old flinty grayness into the look of him. He was surprised when her slim hand dropped lightly on his for a moment.

"I'm sorry," she said simply. "I didn't want to take you back to such days. But there were things I wanted to know. Now let's talk of other things. Of today, for instance. Was there ever a more perfect morning, a more perfect world? Autumn. I remember it back home. So sweetly sad at times, yet so buoyantly wonderful. Out here it is no different, only bigger."

Nothing she might have said could have snapped him more swiftly back to his earlier mood.

"Best season of the year," he enthused. "Hack Asbell put it just about right the other evening when we were having an after-supper smoke out by the corrals. As Hack put it, the time of the year when the earth reaches up and the sky reaches down and a man can listen to the world sing."

"Oh!" she exclaimed. "I like that. Imagine such a crusty old rascal having such nice thoughts! I'll have to know him better."

"That," said Bruce, "is a swell idea. If I should drop around with an extra saddle bronc' someday, would you ride up to headquarters with me?"

"I'd love it!"

"It's a deal. Hack will be tickled out of his skin."

From then on the bars were down. They talked of many things, impersonal things. But Bruce was hugely content. Just to sit there beside her, to watch the sunlight on her hair and the slant of it across her softly sun-browned cheek and throat; to listen to the lilt of her voice and the bright cadence of her occasional laughter. These were things that pushed the gray bleakness of past years away from him.

The miles to Starlight were all too short. She let him off in front of Donovan's store, waited while he untied the reins of the black from the rear of the wagon. Then, with a tip of her hand and a smile, she drove on toward the lumberyard at the far end of town.

Martell went into Donovan's, whistling softly to himself.

From the door of the Land Office, Cashel Edmunds watched all this, then turned and went into the back room of the place. In there was Jason Spelle, dusty and travel-worn, shaving before a small mirror.

"The Carling girl just drove in," Edmunds reported, a malicious glint in his eyes. "Martell rode the wagon with her as far as Donovan's."

The rasp of Spelle's razor paused just a moment. "You figure I'm interested there?" There was no urbanity in Spelle's tone now, instead a thin harshness.

"Used to be, didn't you?"

Spelle whirled. "Don't try and taunt me," he snarled. "You'll find I got answers to a lot of things . . . including you."

Edmunds shrugged in that backing-away, sulky manner of his. "You're sure edgy. A man can't open his mouth."

Spelle turned back, finished his shaving, wiped the remnants of soap from his face with a damp towel. He lifted his shoulder-holstered gun and harness from the back of a chair and buckled it on. He donned his corduroy coat.

Watching him, Cashel Edmunds was uneasy in the change that had come over Spelle. Something that had always been held in check within this man, damped-down and hidden, now had broken loose and was rampant. It put a settled glitter in his eyes, loosened up his mouth, pulled lines into his face. In it was ruthlessness, wildness—and danger. Spelle pulled on his hat and went out without another word.

At the lumberyard, Tracy Carling had turned over her wagon and the list of what she wanted to one of Tom Nixon's men, and now was perched on a pile of sawn lumber, waiting for the loading of her wagon to be done. She was brightly interested in the bustle and industry of the yard, which was a busy place indeed these days, what with all the cabin building going on across the basin. The air smelled of resin and piney sawdust and was a pleasant tang to the nostrils. She was unaware of Spelle's approach until he was right at her elbow and speaking.

"How are you, Tracy?"

"Jason!" She looked at him with wide, startled eyes. "Where in the world have you been?"

He shrugged. "Business. I had finally to look after some affairs of my own."

He looked at her intently, marking her slim grace and shining head with a boldness that made her shift restlessly. "Glad I'm back?"

She stammered slightly. "Why, yes . . . of course."

"Worry about me any?" There was a slight roughness in the words.

Her shoulders stiffened and her head lifted. She looked at him with a sudden cool directness. She did not answer his question. Instead she said: "You've changed, Jason. Your manner . . . your looks."

He laughed curtly. "Naturally. Nothing stands still. All things change, including men. And women."

"What do you mean?"

"You. Grown fond of saddle men . . . maybe?"

She colored sharply, but her manner went cool and proud. "I like neither the tone nor the words," she said stiffly. She slipped down from the lumber pile and would have walked away, but Spelle stepped in front of her, his pale brown eyes moiling. He knew she was angry with him, knew that every additional word he spoke now would make her more so. But the old suave mask was completely gone now, burned away by the wild ruthlessness that had broken loose in him. He caught her by the arm, roughly.

"Not so fast, my lady. Nobody gives Jason Spelle the go-by for a drifting saddle pounder like that damned Martell, that cheap killer."

Tracy went very pale, but her eyes blazed. She saw no handsomeness in this man now, no charm. She saw only an ugliness of spirit that revolted her thoroughly. She tried to twist away from him.

"Let go of me!" she cried. "You complete . . . fool! Let go of me!"

Spelle laughed, his grip tightening. Here was a narrow alley between piles of stacked lumber and, at this moment, empty but for the two of them. Spelle pulled the struggling girl toward him.

One of Tom Nixon's yard hands, a new arrival in the basin and one who had never seen Jason Spelle before, came around a pile of lumber. He saw Tracy Carling trying to pull free of Spelle's grasp, heard her angry, frightened protest. The yardman wasn't particularly quick-witted, but he was a decent and honest man, and one no longer young. He hurried forward.

"Here, you!" he called sharply. "Let go of that girl!"

Spelle cursed, swung around. His lips peeled back and he drove a powerful, wickedly unexpected blow. His fist smashed into the side of the elderly yard hand's face, driving the man heavily against a lumber pile. The man's head thudded against the lumber, his eyes rolled, and he went down in a senseless, bleeding heap.

Tracy was free. She could have run, but she didn't. She stood there, head back and eyes blazing, straight and taut, small fists clenched stiffly at her sides.

Suddenly she wasn't a bit afraid. She was just more furiously angry than she'd ever been before in her life. "You coward!" she flamed. "You . . . you . . . !"

Words choked her. She dropped on her knees beside the unconscious man, pulled a handkerchief from her jacket pocket, and began dabbing at the blood seeping from a corner of the man's mouth. She began to weep softly.

Spelle stared down at her, his mouth ugly. Once he made as if to grab her by the shoulder, but pulled his hand back. The creak of an approaching wagon sounded. Spelle cursed and walked swiftly away.

Tracy kept on weeping. These were tears of anger, more than anything else, burning anger and self-disgust. To think that once she had admired Jason Spelle, believed in him. To think that she had been so completely blind and girlishly silly not to see past the suave mask and recognize what lay beneath it.

That creaking wagon turned into the alley between the lumber piles and came along it. The driver was Kip Martell. From the height of his wagon box, Kip could look over the piled lumber and so saw and recognized the disappearing back of Jason Spelle. And then Kip saw Tracy kneeling beside the beaten yard hand. Kip's wagon was loaded and he was heading back to camp. But now he set his brake, leaped down, and ran ahead.

"Ma'am . . . what happened? How'd the old feller get hurt?"

"A . . . a cowardly brute hit him."

"You mean . . . Jason Spelle clubbed the old feller down?"

Tracy nodded her bright head. "Yes. Jason Spelle."

"But why?"

"Because of me," said Tracy, her lips stiff. "Jason Spelle was becoming . . . offensive. This man interfered and Spelle hit him."

Kip had a canvas water bag slung to his wagon. He got this and sloshed the yard hand's head and face. The man groaned and stirred, his eyes opening. They were vague for a moment, then cleared as they settled on Tracy.

"Miss," he mumbled, "you're all right? That feller . . . ?"

"He's gone," said Tracy quietly. "Thanks to you. And I do thank you."

The yard hand sat up. "That's all right, miss. Glad I happened to come along. Don't you worry about me. I'll be all right."

Tracy stood up. "Thanks again," she said. Then she hurried away. Kip stared after her a moment before turning to the yard hand again.

"Who is she?"

The yard hand shook his head. "Dunno. She come in with a wagon after some lumber. Me and another feller was loading it, over yonder. I come looking for her to tell her the load was ready. I saw her trying to get away from some big guy in a corduroy coat. The youngster was scared and mad. When I moved in, this jigger came around fast and hit me. That's all I know. Thanks for the water."

The yard hand got to his feet, shook his head, and plodded off.

Kip drove his wagon out of the lumberyard and down the street as far as Donovan's. He stopped in front and went in, dug in a pocket for the grub list Cadence Clebourne had given him. From a corner of the store a drawling, familiar voice reached him.

"The old sod-buster himself. How's that cabin coming?"

Kip turned, grinning. "Good enough. Just hauling out the last load of lumber. What you doing in town?"

Bruce came over to him. "Snooping. Keeping an eye on the weather. No more sign of Horgan around?"

"Not since the first day you showed up. I see Jason Spelle is back in circulation."

Interest flashed in Bruce's eyes. "How do you know?"

"Up at the lumberyard. He slugged one of the yard hands. Seems Spelle was pestering a girl who'd ridden in for a load of lumber. This yard hand stepped in and Spelle knocked him cold."

Bruce's voice went brittle. "Who was the girl?"

"Darned if I know. Never saw her before. But

she seemed mighty nice and with awful pretty hair. Why . . . that's her now."

Kip pointed out the door to a wagon rolling past. On the wagon box Tracy Carling sat, her shoulders very straight, her eyes straight ahead. Her face was still slightly pale, her lips tightly locked over disturbing emotions.

Bruce Martell's eyes took on that smoke-dark look, the angles of his face hardening. He started for the door. Kip caught him by the arm. "Where you going?"

"I want a word," said Bruce harshly, "with Mister Jason Spelle."

Bruce went out, with Kip trailing anxiously at his heels. A cold glance showed Bruce that Spelle was nowhere in immediate sight along the street. He went up to the Land Office, where Cashel Edmunds was puttering over some records.

"Spelle," said Bruce. "Where is he?"

Cashel Edmunds was startled at the chill that had come into the office with Bruce Martell. And Edmunds had been ruminating morosely over the contemptuous way Spelle had treated him. Edmunds was afraid of Spelle and he was the sort of individual who, when he feared a man, also came to hate him. Of late, Edmunds had known increasing uneasiness—the threat to put him in the street just as had happened to Dyke and Bully Thorpe if he Edmunds tried to pull out of the original deal they had made. There was a meanness, a smallness, and a lack of courage in Cashel Edmunds. He hated Bruce Martell for the same reason he hated Spelle—because he was afraid of him. But he was smart enough to recognize the darkness of Bruce's mood, and in it he read something that boded no good for Jason Spelle. Here was a weak man's way to hit back. So he answered truthfully.

"I saw him go into The Frontier just a little bit ago."

Bruce went out, headed for The Frontier. Kip tugged at his brother's arm again. "Listen, cowboy . . . what's set you off? You know that girl, maybe?"

"I know her. No finer girl ever breathed. And Spelle . . . why damn his crooked soul . . . !"

He was too full of it to hold it all under cover, this black, bitter rage that had become an ever-increasing torrent in him. Some it broke into the full open with his final words. Kip was awed. But he said: "Right with you, big feller."

They went into The Frontier, side-by-side.

And Cashel Edmunds, locking the door of his office, slipped cautiously toward The Frontier himself.

Jason Spelle was at the bar, tossing off a whiskey. Savage currents were loose in him, too. He was reviewing the sequence of events since he first came into Indio Basin. He had laid his plans carefully, provided for all foreseeable angles. It had been a wicked plan and a ruthless one, but it was big and daring and promised rich gain. In his heart, Jason Spelle had never known anything but contempt for the settlers, the contempt of a ruthless predator for the intended victims. He knew from the first that many of them would be easily swayed, easily led. Even while he murdered and looted the richer camps, he could blind the others by playing on their dislike and suspicion of cattle interests, and so keep them looking along the false finger of blame toward Hack Asbell's Rocking A. And in the end, using the mass of their numbers as a club, he would have the Rocking A, too.

That was how he had figured things, and everything was working smoothly toward this very end, when the one thing he had been unable to provide against took place. A man had ridden into Indio Basin. One man. Bruce Martell. And from the day Martell appeared, the smooth workings of the great idea had begun to falter. Black, murderous hate came easily to a man like Jason Spelle. It was working in him now toward Bruce Martell.

That girl—that fool Carling girl. Sure she was a pretty thing, attractive to any man's eye, and of interest to him, insofar as any girl could interest him. It wasn't, he told himself savagely, that he really gave a thin damn if he ever saw or spoke to her again. No, that wasn't what galled and punished him. It was the fact that here, too, Bruce Martell had become an opposing factor.

Spelle ground his teeth and his eyes pinched to a hardness that made them ache. The little fool! He should have twisted her neck.

Something hard and round and menacing bored against the small of Spelle's back. And a voice, Bruce Martell's voice, laid flat emphasis in his ears.

"Turn around . . . slow."

Spelle turned. Now the muzzle of Bruce Martell's gun prodded him in the pit of the stomach. "Lift your hands."

Spelle licked his lips, cursing himself soundlessly for being so consumed with his raging thoughts as to allow himself to be taken so completely off guard. His pale brown eyes took on a yellowish cast. He lifted his hands.

Bruce shot his free hand up under Spelle's coat, lifted away the shoulder-holstered gun strapped under Spelle's left armpit. He stepped back, handed the gun to Kip.

"All right," he grated harshly. "Now take off your coat. I don't trust a snake like you. There might be a second set of fangs. Take your coat off and drop it."

There was nothing Spelle could do but obey.

"Step away from that bar."

Spelle stepped, and Bruce moved around him, making sure there was no other weapon. Satisfied on this score, Bruce jammed his gun back into the holster, stripped off his gun belt, and handed it to Kip.

"Now," said Bruce flintily, "I make a dirty cur crawl. Coming at you, Spelle."

A raw, savage light flickered in Spelle's eyes as he understood. He was a big man physically in his own right, with plenty of confidence in his ability in a rough-and-tumble, all-out fight. He flexed his arms, clenched his fists, and leaped forward.

They met, he and Bruce Martell, chest to chest, with a crash that shook the room. For a moment or two there were no blows struck. The initial test was one of brute strength, and in this there seemed little to choose. They swayed from side to side, neither winning nor giving an inch. Then, with a hard gust of expelled breath, Spelle loosed one clawing hand and jabbed it forward and up, fingers stiff and spread, aiming at Bruce's eyes.

Bruce got his head back far enough to save his eyes, but Spelle's gouging fingers skidded up his forehead, leaving scalding lines of torn skin and bruised flesh in their wake. He kept on falling back, dragging Spelle with him. Then he pivoted, hard and fast, gaining the leverage to throw Spelle spinning away from him. Spelle smashed into a poker table, which went skidding wildly across the saloon and left Spelle floundering and off balance momentarily.

Bruce went after him, fast, his right fist sailing ahead of him. Spelle threw up a warding arm, partially deflected the blow that otherwise would have found his jaw. As it was, Bruce's fist slammed against the side of Spelle's head and shook him up. Spelle circled, nimble for a big man.

They came together again and Spelle brought up a bunched and driving knee, aiming to disable, then and there. Bruce twisted barely enough to catch the blow on his hip. Then he dropped both hands and pumped them into Spelle's stomach. Spelle grunted and gave ground. Bruce leaped after him and ran into a punch that filled his head with exploding fire. Spelle came at him, whining like a killer jungle cat. Bruce wrapped his arms about his head, covering up, and Spelle stormed all over him, beating at him with both swinging fists.

A stockman with little, hard, flat eyes and a bared head covered with a mop of tightly curled black hair bawled from the end of the bar. "Now you got him, Spelle! Give it to him . . . beat his head off!"

It was Curly Garms, swinging his burly shoulders back and forth, half pumping his heavy arms in unconscious reaction to the fight. Kip Martell, a little taut and white about the lips, shot a glance at Garms and marked him in memory. Then, even as Kip's eyes came back to the battlers, he gave a yelp of delight. For Bruce, crouched and covering, now half straightened and brought a slashing fist up and inside of Spelle's guard. It found Spelle's jaw squarely and Spelle went down in a long, scrambling fall. For a moment he stayed on one knee, shaking a dazed head. Then he was up, pallid with rage and charging in again.

It wasn't good judgment on his part. That punch had slowed his reactions slightly. Now he saw Bruce's fist coming again and he was not fast enough to dodge it or ward it off. It was a wicked blow, with all the drive of Bruce's weight and shoulders behind it. It landed squarely on Spelle's snarling mouth, pulping and crushing. It was the hardest blow of the fight and the most damaging.

Spelle reeled back, his mouth sagging open and spouting crimson. And Bruce went after him mercilessly. Spelle was dazed and sick, his whole lower face feeling paralyzed. Instinctively he raised his arms to ward off another such crushing blow, and that left his body open. Bruce beat at it with thundering fists. A crashing blow under the heart brought Spelle over, gasping. He gave ground faster and faster. A left to the side of his neck spun him half around, and then Bruce cornered him against the bar, knocking him back against it again and again.

Curly Garms began edging in, his black, hard

eyes burning with treacherous purpose. Kip's voice struck at him, bright and cold.

"Get away . . . you! This is a ride Spelle has to make alone. I mean it . . . get away!"

It was Spelle's own gun that Kip was balancing suggestively in his hand, the muzzle bearing on Curly Garms. Garms snarled soundlessly, but he quit trying to edge in.

Spelle couldn't get away from the bar. Each time he tried, Bruce hammered him back. That smash under the heart had weakened Spelle. Now another came thundering in to the same place. His knees began to shake. He was being whipped, whipped by the man who he had come to hate as he had never hated any man before in a lifetime that had seen a great deal of hate. The knowledge sent a new gust of fury burning through him, and he threw himself forward in a wild, crazy rage.

He got a handful of Bruce's shirt and tore the garment clean from him. He tried to claw at Bruce's face again, at his eyes. Bruce beat the hand down with his left fist and threw his right into Spelle's face, a face swollen and blood-smeared and misshapen now. The punch broke the proud arch of Spelle's nose and hung him back over the bar again, shuddering. Spelle's arms began to sink down and Bruce reached past them with a fist that thudded solidly under Spelle's ear.

That was the end of it. Spelle's knees caved.

He spun to face the bar, clawed at its smooth surface, trying to hold himself up. There was no grip on the bar, no strength in his hands. He skidded down the face of the bar, bounced off the brass foot rail, rolled on his face on the floor. He stayed there, retching and shuddering.

Bruce Martell caught up the remnants of his tattered shirt, mopped his face with them. Kip stripped off the denim jumper he was wearing, hung it over Bruce's naked shoulders. Kip's voice was gruff and a trifle choked as he said: "That, big fellah, was one complete and high-class job. Let's get out of here."

The Frontier, with only a scattering of customers when the fight started, was by now jammed to the doors, for the word had spread rapidly and men had come rushing to see. Pat Donovan was there and he fell in on the other side of Bruce as Kip steered a way to the door. Pat was so excited his nearly forgotten Irish brogue broke loose in a torrent.

The crowd gave back, letting them through in silence. There were some ominous looks thrown at Bruce, but even in these there was a grudging aspect. Jason Spelle was still on the floor, after Bruce was gone, and the crowd closed in to stare.

Chapter Nineteen

The period of one big, ripe, golden autumn moon was passed. Now the nights were deeply dark and chill. Chill enough for a fire to feel good in the lath-and-tar-paper shanty where gaunt old Ezra Banks sat, smoking his pipe. A small lamp on the table at his elbow filled the single room with a dim yellow glow. Ezra was ruminating over the news he'd heard that afternoon in town. The news of the meeting between Bruce Martell and Jason Spelle in The Frontier.

Two days previous it had happened, so Pat Donovan had said. Memory of the fight still brightened Pat's eyes. Never, so the storekeeper had declared, had he seen any man so completely whipped as was Jason Spelle.

"That Bruce Martell," ended Donovan. "What a broth of a lad he is. Sure, and Jason Spelle will never be the same after that licking."

Here and there, Ezra had picked up rumors of the cause. Some of these made sense, some did not. But the one that intrigued Ezra most was a chance remark he overheard, uttered by a worker from the lumberyard, an elderly man with the darkness of a bruise staining one side of his face.

"It was over before I could get there," this man

was telling another. "Which I'll always regret, for I'd 'a' give my right arm to have seen that feller Spelle get it, after him smashing me the way he did. Now it wasn't because Spelle hit me that this feller Martell crawled his frame, because Martell don't know me from shucks. So it must have been because Martell knew that girl Spelle was pesterin'. And she was a mighty nice girl, too, with the prettiest hair I ever saw."

Shrewd old Ezra could make plenty of this, so, coming back from town, he cut around by the Carling camp. Here, while making small talk, he had studied Tracy Carling covertly. There was a tautness in her, a deep-seated anger. Presently Ezra managed to get her aside.

"Things happened in town a couple of days ago, so I hear," he said artlessly. "You heard about it, youngster?"

"I heard," answered Tracy curtly. "And I feel all dirtied up. I never want to see Bruce Martell or . . . or that man Spelle again. The idea . . . the two of them beating each other like brute beasts . . . over me. And in a saloon . . . too. I'm . . . I'm disgusted with them and with myself."

"Well, now," Ezra said, "I wouldn't feel that way. Spelle had that whipping coming and Martell gave it to him. I bet Spelle never tries to bother you again. Ain't every girl's got a champion like Bruce Martell."

Tracy made a violent gesture with a small,

clenched fist. "You don't understand. I tell you I never want to see either of them again."

"Likely," said Ezra, old and wise, "you'll change your mind on that, youngster. You want to remember, this is a new country and still a wild one. Men settle their affairs here different than that quiet farm country back where you come from. And no good woman should ever feel ashamed because a good man throws a solid fist for her. If I know Bruce Martell, he won't ever mention it to you, and he won't expect no thanks, nor want any. But don't you hold it ag'in' him for what he did. That wouldn't be fair."

To which Tracy stamped her foot and turned her back on him.

Later, sitting quietly in his cabin, Ezra chuckled over the memory. A proud youngster, that Tracy girl.

A knock sounded at the door, startling, because Ezra had heard no sound of outside approach. He threw a glance toward his bunk along the far wall, at the old trunk shoved back beneath it. Hanging on a couple of pegs above the bunk was an old Spencer carbine.

The knock came again, with a peculiar insistence about it. Ezra got up quietly, moved over until he had only to reach an arm to lift the old rifle free. Then he boomed: "Come in!"

The door swung back and Ezra grabbed for the Spencer. For the faint glow of the lamplight, reaching beyond the open door, showed a figure masked to the eyes behind a bandanna handkerchief.

Ezra had the Spencer free and half lifted when a harsh curse spat at him from behind that masking handkerchief. A curse and the words: "No you don't!"

Then gun flame bloomed through the door, feral red and lancing. Ezra Banks never felt the lead smash into him. He never knew what hit him. He just fell sideways, half on his bunk, half off it. That quickly could the bridge between life and death be crossed.

The masked killer came in, followed by two others. "The damned old fool," snarled the killer. "He would have it."

"No matter," said one of the others. "These sodbusters are just a bunch of sheep. The money is around here somewhere. Let's get about locating it. We got a big night ahead."

They found the money, in the trunk under the bunk. They took it and rode away. They didn't bother to close the door. And later, when a chill night wind began to drift across the earth's blackness, the push of it swung the door back and forth in a dismal creaking.

Not long after, across the half mile run of country where the Carling camp lay, another shot sounded. And after that the tattoo of racing hoofs, speeding away and fading into the night.

Up at the Rocking A headquarters, Bruce Martell arose in a gray, chill dawn and dressed to the discomfort of muscles still creaking stiffly to remind him of the fight now a few days past. In an all-out mix-up like that, he thought grimly, a man never realized how much he'd put out or how much he'd taken until after the muscular reaction came.

He stepped into the bite of the outer air and went over to the cook shack. Water he poured into the tin basin on the bench beside the door, then shoveled with cupped hands across his face, made him gasp with its iciness. But the rough toweling brought an answering glow, and morning hunger leaped up in him.

Back by the corrals, hoofs clumped. Bruce turned and stared. It was a heavy work horse, coming at an unaccustomed, weary jog, and on its broad back a slim figure was hunched. Even in the dawn's mistiness there could be no mistake. Bruce hurried over at a run.

"Tracy! You? Girl . . . what's wrong?"

She pulled to a halt. Her face was ghostly pale, twisted with grief and terror, her eyes wide and stunned. She stared at Bruce as though from a great distance and spoke tonelessly through stiff lips.

"Uncle Brink . . . they shot him. They smashed our wagons, robbed us. Ezra Banks . . . Ezra . . . he's dead."

She spoke droningly, mechanically, as though all emotion and feeling were frozen in her. Only her hands moved, fingers twisting and untwisting in the ragged mane of the stolid old work horse.

"Girl," cried Bruce softly. "What are you talking about? You can't mean . . . ?"

She began to sway, and suddenly she was toppling off her mount. Bruce caught her in his arms, and she lay in them, still and white.

Bruce carried her over to Hack Asbell's cabin, kicked open the door, his voice lashing ahead of him. "Hack! Up and out, Hack. Here's trouble . . . plenty!"

The old cattleman had just awakened. He came up in his blankets, blinking stupidly. He began to swear.

"What the hell . . . ?"

"It's Tracy Carling," cut in Bruce savagely. "She brings word of dead men and robbery down in the basin. Hurry up . . . get into your clothes!"

As soon as Asbell was out of his bunk, Bruce lowered the girl onto it, smoothing the blankets under her. Asbell dressed, bent over the girl, touching one of her hands.

"Here . . . ," he rasped, "get a blanket over her. She's half frozen. Where's that whiskey bottle?"

He got the bottle and Bruce edged a little of the liquor through the girl's lips. She choked a little, moaned, opened her eyes. Asbell pushed Bruce aside.

"Here, let me handle this, son."

The girl stared around, that stunned, stricken look in her eyes. Hack Asbell sat on the edge of the bunk, holding one of her chilled hands between both his gnarled palms.

"It's me, lass," he said gently. "Old Hack Asbell. Now what's this you've come to tell us?"

She struggled to a sitting position. Suddenly with a little gasping cry she caught at him and began to sob wildly. Old Hack wrapped both arms about her and she clung to him, crying in a way that tore and wrenched at Bruce Martell's heart in a savage agony. Hack Asbell held her gently, crooning soft words.

"There . . . there, youngster. It's all right. Have your cry and then tell old Hack all about it."

Her period of wild grief was as short as it was violent. Presently she began to quiet and Hack eased her back onto the pillow. "Now, youngster . . . tell us about it."

She did, haltingly at first, then with the words breaking from her almost in a torrent. Bruce stood, tall and dark and still, his face a taut mask, missing no word.

In the Carling camp, it seemed, they had just turned in for the night. Then there was the sound of hoofs, coming toward their camp. Brink Carling got up, to greet whoever it was riding in. Riders barged in suddenly, masked riders. One of them tried to club Brink Carling down with a swinging gun. Carling struggled with the fellow, who pulled away and shot him. Then the raiders began ransacking the camp. There was quite a bit of money hidden in the big wagon. The raiders tore everything to pieces before they found it. Then, with the camp axe, one of them deliberately wrecked the big wagon and the spring wagon, smashing spokes from the wheels. Then they raced away into the night again.

Both Tracy and Aunt Lucy thought at first that Brink Carling was dead. He wasn't, but he was badly wounded. Aunt Lucy was caring for him as best she could. Tracy caught up one of the heavy work horses and rode over to Ezra Banks's camp for help. And she found Ezra Banks lying dead in his cabin. Her next thought for help was the Rocking A. She knew she could find the head-quarters if she just took the trail and stayed on it. She didn't know why she had come here instead of going to town for help. It was just something inside her, something instinctive that told her to come to the Rocking A.

"You did right, youngster," said Hack Asbell, harshness coming into his tone. "Now you just rest a little and we'll take care of everything." He looked up at Bruce. "You and the boys will ride, of course, son. Every man with a rifle under his leg and guns at his belt. Lord knows I'm no savior of other people . . . but a thing like this! Bruce . . . get those damn' murdering raiders . . .

get 'em any way you can. I'll take care of the youngster here. I'll hook up a rig and get right down to the Carling camp and take over there. But you ride. I don't care how far or how long, but bring me the ears of those dirty whelps!"

Bruce looked down at the girl's haunted eyes and quivering lips. He said: "Glad you made it an order, Hack. Because I'd have gone, anyhow."

He whirled and went out. His harsh yell emptied the bunkhouse, brought the crew into the cook shack. While they gulped hot coffee, he told them the story. He saw gray anger break in every one of them.

"God knows," exploded Carp Bastion, "I've never loved any sod-buster. But murder is murder. This is our chore, Bruce."

Butte Allen said: "There'll be some ready to believe Rocking A responsible. We can prove different by dragging in those responsible, dead or alive. What're we waiting for?"

"Not a thing," rapped Bruce. "Saddle and ride!" He turned to the cook. "Take a mug of this coffee over to Hack's cabin, Muley. That girl needs it."

Five minutes later, in a thunder of hoofs, Rocking A started its ride of retribution.

At Hack Asbell's urging, Tracy Carling drank the coffee that Muley brought. Asbell drew the cook aside.

"Go hook a team to my buckboard, Muley.

While I'm gone, you give this cabin a mucking out and bring in a couple more bunks. There's a badly wounded man I'm going to bring here, along with his wife and this girl. They'll be staying for a while. And put a big bundle of blankets in the back of the buckboard. And Muley, keep that old buffalo Sharps rifle of yours handy. Should any riding bunch outside our own boys start coming into headquarters, you start shooting . . . for keeps."

Muley, a gruff, bearded old fellow who limped on a crooked leg, nodded. "I heard what Bruce told the gang. I'll shoot, and I won't miss, Hack."

Bruce Martell led his men straight to the Carling camp. Six riders besides himself. There was Carp Bastion and Butte Allen. Jim Lark and Speck Morrison. Card Wilcox and Rowdy Turner. Good men, all, when headed right. And tough in a fight.

The Carling camp looked much the same, except that both the heavy and the spring wagons sagged drunkenly, because of smashed wheels. There was a fire going and Brink Carling lay beside it, blanketed. His wife crouched beside him.

Bruce took off his hat as he rode up. Every man with him did the same. The look on Aunt Lucy's face cut Bruce like a knife. Her fine, brave eyes held the same wide, stricken look as had been in Tracy's. Bruce spoke gently.

"Brink . . . he's still alive, Missus Carling?" He held his breath for her answer. He marveled at the low steadiness of it.

"Yes. Still alive. With help . . . I've hopes."

"Hack Asbell is on his way, bringing Tracy with him. Hack will take care of everything. Now I wonder . . . was there any chance of recognizing any of those devils who did this thing? Any voice . . . anything at all that you remember?"

She seemed to consider. Then her white head shook. "It was dark, and Brink was down. . . . There were so many of them."

"At a rough guess . . . how many, Missus Carling?"

"I . . . don't know. Ezra Banks . . . Tracy told you about Ezra?"

"Yes, she told us. We'll make this all up to you, Missus Carling. And remember, Hack will be here shortly. Is there anything we can do . . . right now?"

"Nothing. I've done all that can be done for . . . for Brink. The bleeding has stopped. There's more color in his face." She leaned over and ran a gentle hand across the blanketed figure beside her.

At the gesture, Carp Bastion groaned. "And to think I once tried to get rough in this camp! Butte, when this chore is over, if I'm still alive, back me up against the corral fence and work me over with a pick handle. As a personal favor, Butte."

"That goes for both of us, Carp," answered

Butte. "I was here, too, wasn't I? Right now I see myself as knee-high to a grasshopper."

The other riders were stirring restlessly when Bruce Martell swung his horse back to join them. "This way!" he ordered, and spurred off toward Ezra Banks's cabin.

The lamp had burned itself out. Ezra Banks lay, a gaunt and shrunken figure. Bruce stood for a moment in the doorway, then went back to his saddle.

"Had to make sure old Ezra was past help," he told the crew bleakly. "Now . . . town."

Carp Bastion swung his head. "You figure to find those raiders in town, Bruce?"

"No. But their trail, maybe. Come on!"

They went into Starlight in a compact group. The town was boiling with feeling. Settlers along the street glowered and cursed, but offered nothing worse against this grim, heavily armed little band of riding men. Bruce went into the store alone. Donovan was there, talking to Pete Martin and Sam Otten. They were grave and bleak of face. They became more so when Bruce told about Ezra Banks and Brink Carling. Donovan shook his head dolefully.

"That makes six camps raided that I know of, Bruce. Maybe word of more will come in later. This is the worst I ever heard of. I'm no fighting man, but right now I could be dangerous if I knew which way to look."

"We're thinking of calling a mass meeting," said Sam Otten. "Something has got to be done."

"Something will be done, Sam," Bruce declared. "Rocking A is riding, as soon as we know which way to ride. Those murdering whelps must have left a trail somewhere. And there's another angle."

"What's that?" demanded Pete Martin.

Bruce built a smoke. He spoke slowly, with frowning concentration. "It's just an idea of mine I've been mulling over. See what you think of it. I came into this basin owing allegiance to no one but myself. I was neither a settler nor part of the Rocking A. My mind was open. What did I find? I found a blind hatred on the part of virtually all the settlers against saddle men . . . any saddle man. I couldn't figure it. Most of these settlers were solid men, not of the drifting, haywire, shiftless squatter type who instinctively hate cattle interests and riding men, blaming them for all past and present misfortunes. It didn't add up in my mind that a single cattle outfit, Rocking A, could have antagonized all these settlers in the short space of a few weeks. So what did I find? I found that one man, Jason Spelle, was responsible for most of that ill feeling. He had settled on no land himself, so it wasn't possible that Rocking A had ever done anything to him personally to arouse his hate. But Spelle was riding every-where across the basin, preaching that hate to the settlers. So I wondered about that."

He paused, inhaling deeply. "Two settler camps were raided, two men killed and robbed. Hendee and Dopkins. Evidence was left at each camp, pointing to the Rocking A as being responsible. I believe I proved to you men and others that Rocking A was not responsible. But somebody was. Now then . . . we know both men were robbed. Who could have known both had large sums of money? Only someone who had visited these men, talked with them, gained their confidence, and got them to talk of their future plans."

Sam Otten caught his breath. "Spelle, maybe?"

Bruce jerked his head. "Spelle. No other. Well?"

Pete Martin took a short turn up and down, his deep eyes beginning to burn. "Logical thinking," he admitted growlingly. "Go on."

"Spelle refused to admit the evidence of Rocking A's innocence in the Hendee and Dopkins affairs . . . refused flatly, even though it was conclusive. He still went on with his damned lying preaching against us. I called him on it and he backed down. Right after that the Thorpes made their try to get me. Which could have been their own idea, though somehow I don't think so. Anyway, after that try went sour, Jason Spelle dropped from sight for some little time. He comes back with all his old smooth gloss missing. There's something loose in him that he'd kept controlled and hidden, before.

There was ugliness in him. There was cause for me to muss him up some. He disappears once more. And then . . . there was last night. So, I'm plenty interested in finding out just where Mister Jason Spelle is now."

"And if you found him, you figger you might learn some of the answers about last night?" asked Pete Martin.

"That's right."

"Where do you intend to start looking?" asked Sam Otten.

"Spelle and Cashel Edmunds were always pretty thick," Bruce answered. "I'm going to have a talk with Edmunds. Want to come along?"

"Why not?" growled Pete Martin, heading for the door, "Now that you mention it, Bruce . . . you may have something there."

To his men, as he and Martin and Otten and Pat Donovan went along the store porch, Bruce said: "Stay put. I'll be right back."

The Land Office was empty, but there were sounds of movement in the back room. Without ceremony, Bruce shoved open the door to that room and led the way in. Cashel Edmunds was there, alone. On the bunk stood an open grip sack. Edmunds was shoving odds and ends of clothes into it. He came around, fast and startled at the interruption and at sight of the grim group facing him, his eyes flickered and went shifty. He tried to cover up with bluster.

"I do business in the front office. These are my private living quarters. You got no right to bust in here uninvited."

Bruce looked at the grip sack. "Going someplace, maybe?"

"If I am," Edmunds retorted, "that's my business and none of yours."

"That's where you're wrong, Edmunds," snapped Pete Martin. "Your business is our business, right now. Where's Jason Spelle?"

Edmunds's shiftiness grew. "How would I know?" he muttered sulkily. "I'm not Spelle's keeper."

"Maybe not," put in Pat Donovan. "But I'm remembering that you and Spelle were always pretty thick, and that he generally hung around the Land Office a lot when he was in town."

"That still don't mean anything to me," Edmunds said. He made as if to shut the grip sack, but Bruce Martell was there first, shoving him aside.

"Just for the hell of it," said Bruce coldly, "I'm going to take a look."

He began emptying the grip sack on the bunk. Edmunds shrilled at him.

"Damn you, Martell . . . keep your paws off my things. You got no right. . . ."

"This day I'm making a lot of things my right. Ah! What's this?"

It was a canvas sack, folded and tied around a

fairly thick wad of something jammed into the bottom of the sack. Bruce loosened the tie, opened the sack, upended it, and shook it. A solid wad of currency fell from it, scattered on the bunk. Only a casual glance was enough to tell that here were several thousands of dollars.

"Edmunds," said Bruce, "you travel well-heeled."

One of the bills, a twenty, missed the bunk and fluttered to the floor. Sam Otten moved to pick it up. He stiffened, stared at what he held. His eyes went hard and spots of color leaped into his face. Bruce, noting this, asked sharply. "What's the matter, Sam?"

Otten answered slowly, as though weighing every word, weighing them as if he realized that on every one of them might mean a man's life.

"I could be mistaken, understand . . . or it could be coincidence. As you know, Jake Hendee was a neighbor of mine. He had an extra plow that I could use. I made a deal with him and bought it, paying sixty dollars for it. I paid him with three twenty dollar bills. Before I paid him, we both worked at cleaning some axle grease off the share of the plow. And when I paid him, I got a smear of grease on one of the bills. I was willing to dig up another, but Jake said a little grease wouldn't hurt the value of the bill. So he took it. And . . . well . . . !"

Otten held up the bill and the dark stain of

grease on it was plain to all. Pat Donovan said: "There's all kinds of grease, Sam . . . but I know axle grease and the smell of it. I sell enough of it, so I ought to know. Let's see that."

Donovan took the bill, looked closely at the stain, smelled it. "Axle grease, right enough," he said curtly.

Had Cashel Edmunds kept his mouth shut, they would still have had nothing concrete against him. For in a land of wagon men there could be plenty of grease-stained currency floating around. But a great and terrifying fear was surging in Edmunds, rattling and confusing him.

"Sure I got that bill from Hendee," he blustered, sweat beginning to bead his face. "I remember it. It was part of his recording and filing fee."

Sam Otten's stubborn jaw pushed out. "Edmunds, you're lying. Jake Hendee had done his recording and filing a good week before I bought the plow from him. You've either talked too much or not enough."

"Right," growled Pete Martin. "And if that bill was paid you for a recording and filing fee, why is it here in your private grip sack, instead of in the safe in the office out front? Who are you working for, anyhow . . . the government or yourself?"

"You forget, gentlemen," put in Bruce with biting sarcasm, "that Mister Edmunds has all the earmarks of making ready for a hurried and extensive journey . . . somewhere."

"He'll make an extensive journey, all right," exploded Pete Martin. "All we have to do is see to it that this little story reaches the street and the settler men along it. In which case Mister Edmunds would take a very long journey, and his last one, on the end of a rope. Bruce, I think the logic of your reasoning is sound. We've run into something."

Desperation flared in Edmunds's eyes. He made a dive for the end of the bunk, grappled under the blankets and was coming up with a snub-nosed gun when Bruce pounced on him. Bruce tore the gun away from him, slammed him against the wall of the room so violently the whole building shook.

"Edmunds," Bruce rasped. "You better talk and talk fast. And straight. Where's Jason Spelle?"

Cashel Edmunds was of weaker fiber than they dreamed. He went all to pieces suddenly. He began to curse wildly, and he was cursing Jason Spelle. When this tempest ran out of him, he was panting and sweating and pallid.

"Spelle," he gulped. "That damned Spelle. He's crazy . . . stark crazy, I tell you . . . since that beating you gave him. I told him to go slow. I told him I wanted no part of his doings . . . and he threatened to kill me. Sure I was with him . . . up to a certain point. I was with him against the Rocking A. We had a deal there . . . to bust Hack Asbell and take over ourselves. With enough settlers hating Rocking A and backing our hand, we figured to be able to do that. But this other stuff . . . this killing and robbing . . . that was Spelle's and Horgan's idea. Spelle and Horgan's gang did all that. I've never moved a step out of this town since the land rush began. You can't tie me in with the killings."

"Yet," reminded Bruce remorselessly, "we find some of the money taken from a murdered man in your possession. How do you explain that, Edmunds?"

Edmunds dropped to the end of the bunk, shaking. The terror of the man came out of him like an odor, offensive and disgusting. Pete Martin would have said something, but a jerk of Bruce's head kept him silent.

"We'll say you had no actual hand in those raids, Edmunds," Bruce said sternly. "We'll say that because of that, there's a thin chance of you getting off with a whole skin, even though you're a slimy, low-lived, conniving skunk. But you win that chance only, if you tell me what I mainly want to know. Spelle and Horgan and the rest of those raiders . . . they must have a hide-out somewhere. All right, Edmunds . . . where?"

Edmunds clasped his hands, twisting them. "I don't know, for sure. That's God's truth, Martell. But I've heard some talk about a place called Loco Mono Creek. East, somewhere."

"Ha!" exclaimed Pat Donovan. "There is such a

place. Loco Mono . . . Crazy Monkey Creek. I've heard of it. Some of your Rocking A men should know about it, Bruce."

Bruce turned to the door. "Then it's time to be moving. I leave this rat to you men. Do as you want with him. Only remember . . . he did talk."

"He'll be here when you get back, Bruce," boomed Pete Martin. "This is the concern of every decent man in Indio Basin. And we'll let them decide. It will be a fair trial, with all angles weighed. Good luck."

Rocking A was still waiting down in front of the store. They looked at Bruce inquiringly as he stepped into his saddle.

"A creek," said Bruce. "Loco Mono Creek. Where is it?"

"East," answered Carp Bastion. "A good fifteen miles. Where Hayfork River runs through some badlands. Loco Mono Creek comes into the river there. What about it?"

"We're riding for it, Carp. Somewhere around there is the hang-out of them we want."

Chapter Twenty

They rode steadily but not too fast. Fifteen miles was fifteen miles and there was no telling exactly what lay at the end of them—perhaps the need of a reserve of strength and speed in their horses. On these a great deal could depend. And so they kept a pace that covered ground reasonably well, but which did not drag too much from their mounts.

They passed settler camps on their way, but they rode wide around these. With the word of what had taken place the previous night spreading across the basin, there was no telling when some enraged settler might go berserk and start sniping with a rifle at any man or group of men sitting saddles.

But as the miles dropped behind, settler camps grew fewer and fewer until finally the run of the surrounding country lay empty of any sign of them. Moving up beside Bruce, Carp Bastion explained why.

"Hungry land we're gettin' into, Bruce. Notice how thin the grass is here? This stretch of land is one part of Indio Basin that ain't worth a damn. In the old days when we run cattle in the basin, you couldn't keep 'em on this grass. There's nothin' to it. And them sod-busters don't want no part of this land, either. This is the edge of the badlands country. Pretty soon there'll be low ridges pushing up, rocky and worthless and just takin' up good space. Them ridges run every which way. Hayfork River cuts right through the middle of 'em and Loco Mono Crick drops in from the north about halfway along. Now that I've started to think about it, I don't know of a place within a hundred miles where a bunch of wild ones could have a hide-out camp and run less chance of being found. A smart one must have picked it."

Sure, mused Bruce, a smart one. Like Jason Spelle. Who didn't overlook a single angle except the most important one of all—and that was that other men could think, could add and subtract, could judge cause and effect, weigh motives, and apply logic. It was, he thought with grim satisfaction, a failing common to the crooked mind, this illusion that only they, the crooked ones, were smart, that and their overlooking the fact that in every chain there would be one link weaker than all the rest, and that sometimes this link could be broken, as Cashel Edmunds had broken. Well, the answer to it all was not too far away.

The land began to take on a persistent upward slope, gradual and long-running. The rolling smoothness gave way to shallow gulches, twisting and winding. In one of these, deep enough to hide a horseman, Bruce drew rein, began building a smoke.

"We don't know a damned thing of what we may find, if anything," he said. "It won't do to go barging around in a bunch. We're not an army. Chances are they could outnumber us. Unless they're stupider than I think, they'll have guards out. We get spotted, we can ride right into a tight that'll get us all shot out of our saddles. From here on in it's slow and careful. So far, I haven't seen a single hoof mark leading into this country. And that's what I want to find, a trail of some sort, with sign on it to read. Might as well light down right here and talk this over."

This they did, hunkering on their boot heels. Butte Allen drawled: "All the way from town I've been thinking, Bruce. About if Loco Mono is the country that gang hangs out in, then they must have a certain way in and out that they favor. I don't think it would be from the west side. It's good land on the west side, with plenty of settler camps scattered around. These settlers would be sure to hear horses pounding by at night, which would be a tip-off. So, it stands to reason the raiders would use some other way, either some-where along here at the middle, or around at the east end of the roughs. As you say, we've seen no bronco sign around here, so that leaves the east end as our most likely chance of finding what we want. What do you think?"

"I think smooth headwork, Butte. The raiders know they can't ride without leaving sign, but they can also make that sign look like it's heading somewhere it ain't. Like if they were to break straight east, pretty well south of Hayfork River, it could look like they were coming in and out from clear back at War Lance Creek, where the jump-off started. But once they get far enough east, they could then cut north and come around into these roughs. Was I heading a gang like that, I'd probably figure that should be the safe angle."

Carp Bastion, restless, impatient, said: "Let's get down that way and have a look."

"No," said Bruce. "We stay right here until dusk. Then we move. Only we don't go in by the way we figure the raiders do. That's the side they'll be guarding. So we come in from the west. How do you figure we stand here? Are we as far along as where Loco Mono Creek comes into the river?"

Both Carp and Butte shook their heads. "I'd say that, were we to hit due north from here, we'd hit the river a good two miles west of Loco Mono," said Carp.

"Two, maybe three," agreed Butte.

"Fine," said Bruce. "Come dusk, we cut straight for the river, then work down it to Loco Mono. And we'll see what we see. Might as well unsaddle, boys. Here's where we wait for sundown."

227

"Huh!" grunted Carp. "We wait until dark and do locate the camp, by that time they'll be out on another raid, and that'll leave us holding the sack."

"I don't think so," differed Bruce. "I doubt they'd raid again tonight. They'll know they left a hornet's nest behind 'em from last night. From now on, for a time at least, settlers will be sleeping plenty light and ready to shoot at the first sound of a horse. The raiders know that. I think they'll figure to let things quiet down a little before hitting again. And if we find their camp, and it's empty, we'll just lie around and wait for them to come back. Keep your shirt on, Carp. Riding wild and blind can do us more harm than good."

So that was the way it was. They unsaddled and lounged the hours away.

"Should have brought some grub along," grumbled Carp once. "Just that cup of java we got outside of this mornin' is damn' thin day-long fare for a healthy man. I'm hungry enough to eat a snake."

"I ain't thinking about anything else but getting somebody in that gang over the sights of a gun," said Rowdy Turner. "I want to see him fold over and kick. Damn a whelp who murders men in the dark. I wonder how that sod-buster, Carling, is making out?"

Bruce, stretched flat on his back, hat over his eyes to shield out the pale autumn sun, was wondering the same thing. And wondering about Tracy, and Aunt Lucy. He wondered if he'd ever get the sound of Tracy's racking grief out of his ears, or forget the look of Aunt Lucy as she crouched alone beside her wounded husband, gently stroking the blankets covering him. He knew just how Rowdy Turner felt, knew the same raw hunger for vengeance. Given the right break, he told himself savagely, he'd lay a terrible lesson this night, for all raiders and outlaws to study for a long time to come.

He wondered why he seemed fated to things of this sort. Rawhide, Ravensdale—now Indio Basin. Back there it had been behind a badge. Out here the badge was missing, but the purpose and the need were the same. Maybe it wasn't fate at all. Maybe it was something inside himself, something that rose up inside him and challenged him to action. Carp Bastion was no more impatient to get about this business than he was himself. But brains, he knew, had won more fights than gunfire. Common sense said to hold this thing off until dark. So that was the way it would be.

The sun arched and fell away, sliding toward a sunset of blazing color. Shadows began to pile up in these shallow gulches. Haze settled down like chill, powder-blue smoke. Bruce got his saddle and went over to his horse.

They lined away in single file up the gulch. Ahead, in the far distance, the Lodestones piled up, blue-black and cold-looking. When the gulch funneled up to a ridge point, Bruce looked west and saw—just a faint spark across the miles—a settler fire begin to glow.

Full dark pushed dusk out of the way rapidly. It was slow going for the Rocking A crew. Carp hadn't exaggerated when he said this would be rough and broken country. It was knobbed and ridged, pitching up and down steeply. One moment Bruce and his men would be up on some star-touched ridge. Then they would be riding through some velvet-black gulch. They circled some points, sent their horses, grunting and scrambling, over others. But always the way was north.

Abruptly the air took on a damp smell, the smell of the river. They found a break in a low rimrock, went slithering down the slide of talus below. Here was a low, narrow bench land, with the river water hissing softly over a riffle threading a mass of scrub willow.

Now they turned east. They rode slowly, taut and tall in their saddles, every sense stretched and alert. This bench they were on followed the river steadily, guarded by the low rim. In places it narrowed to only a few yards, in others the rim swooped back to lay the freedom of comparatively spacious flats. In one place where the bench narrowed, Bruce Martell reined in and left his saddle. And then, crouched low and shielding the faint light of a match behind his hat, searched the width of the bench. Nowhere was its thin grass trampled, or the earth gouged by the hoofs of horses. There was no trail here.

They went on and now Butte Allen moved up beside Bruce. He pointed a long arm. Ahead and on the far side of the river loomed the dark mass of a humpback ridge, running down out of the Lodestone foothills from the north.

"On the far side of that ridge . . . Loco Mono Crick," he murmured. "If those *hombres* are around, we ought to know it pretty quick."

They eased ahead. Bruce listened so intently a singing sound set up in his ears, maybe the whine of his own pulse. But it wasn't by sound or sight that the warning came. It came through another sense. Bruce caught a whiff of wood smoke.

He reined in again. He murmured orders in the softest of voices. He stepped out of the saddle and slid his rifle from its scabbard. The rest followed suit. He ordered Card Wilcox to stay with the horses, to that quiet cowboy's huge disgust. They took off their spurs, hung them on saddle horns. Then they went on, following that scent of wood smoke drifting along the river.

Here the pressure of the rim on the south and the down-thrusting snout of the ridge on the north crowded the channel of the river to a narrowness that built up a foaming rapid filling the night with chill spray and a solid, booming voice that muted everything of lesser extent.

Bruce and his men made the most of this welcome overtone of rumbling waters. They felt their way past spray-wet boulders and splashed, boot deep, through the water between. As abruptly as this gorge had narrowed, it spread wide again into a willow-mottled flat. Here the smell of wood smoke was very strong and here, glowing through a masking line of willow, loomed the crimson of a fire. And from somewhere beyond came the stamp of a weary horse.

Drawing his men close about him, Bruce whispered his plan of battle. Butte Allen, Rowdy Turner, and Speck Morrison around the right-hand end of the willow fringe. Himself and Carp Bastion and Jim Lark around the left-hand end.

"I'll give them the chance to give up quietly. If they don't take it, well . . . they've asked for it."

Now it was on hands and knees, then flat on their bellies, edging carefully along, pushing their rifles ahead of them. It was work to set a knot in a man's stomach, make the hair on the back of his neck bristle, so taut and biting was the tension. Discovery at this point could spoil everything, for it was only a stride or two from firelight to complete darkness, and if they won those two strides, then the shadowy figures lounging around the blaze would be gone like flushed quail. And in this wilderness and outer dark, who could follow successfully?

Bruce thought he never would get past the end

of the willows. Yet he did, finally, and peered through the partial screen of the last sagging branch.

Pitch Horgan he saw and recognized. And that lanky, gangling, hatchet-faced one beside him was Whip Thorpe, who had seen his brothers die on the street of Starlight and who had fled the scene in terror. But here he was, part of this dark and vicious gang, who struck in the dark and killed and robbed and despoiled. There were others Bruce did not recognize until he saw, a little farther back than the rest, a round, bullet head, thick-hatched with curly black hair. Curly Garms. Garms—who had walked among other settlers and proclaimed their cause as his—a traitor of the lowest sort.

But where was Spelle? The one man above all others that Bruce wanted. Bruce, again, went over those he could see. There were some who lounged full length and of these Bruce could not be sure. One of them might be Spelle.

The camp was quiet. Only now and then did an occasional growling remark fall. There was a blackened coffee pot tucked close to the fire. Now Pitch Horgan, squatting before it, leaned over, poured some of the liquid into a cup, then hunkered back, nursing the cup between curved hands. He sipped from it, cursed harshly as the scalding liquid seared his tongue.

At the far end of the willow fringe a stick

cracked sharply. Horgan whirled, alert as a wolf. "What was that?" he rapped. "Who's out there?"

"Ease up, Pitch," said Curly Garms. "You're spooky as hell. Nothin' out there. You're still thinkin' of last night."

"You're damn' right I am," retorted Horgan. "I ain't takin' no chances, in spite of what you and Spelle say. This place is a good hide-out camp, all right. But it could be a trap, too."

Curly Garms laughed. "You leave things up to Jason. He's nobody's fool. I know. I've worked with him a long time. He shoots square with them who work with him and he divvies even. You'll get your share of what he drags out of that Land Office safe tonight. He'll bring Edmunds's share along with him, after he gets done with that damn' spineless whelp. And we'll get our cut apiece out of what Edmunds had. Jason knows what he's doin'."

"Mebbe so," said another of the gang, getting to his feet. "Just the same, Pitch is believing me when I say nothing is certain or safe as long as that Bruce Martell *hombre* is anywhere around. I can't make the rest of you understand what that means. But I'm remembering Rawhide and Ravensdale. If you jingoes had been around those towns when Martell was working 'em, you'd be wiser men."

Garms said, still jibing: "You'll be seein' ghosts

yet, Brazos. Speakin' of Martell, when you makin' another try for that brother of his, Pitch? Or have you given up that idea?"

"Next raid night we call on him," growled Horgan. "I ain't givin' up nothin'. Lip Matole was a good friend of mine. Young Martell downed him, and I'm goin' to even up for Lip."

Brazos, still on his feet and listening carefully, drew a gun and started to prowl toward the far end of the willow fringe. "I'm taking a look, Pitch," he said.

Bruce Martell's voice cut across the night like a keen-edged knife. "You'll stop where you are, Brazos. Bruce Martell talking. We're all around you. Don't anybody move."

For a moment nobody did, frozen stark with surprise. Then, with a turn of his hand, Pitch Horgan upset the contents of his coffee cup into the heart of the fire, and the glow of it was diminished a good third in the wink of an eye. Then Horgan was clawing his way back toward the shadows, dragging at his gun.

He never made it. Someone at the far end of the willow fringe shot at the same moment Bruce did. The bullets crossed in Horgan's body and he went down in a heap. Brazos didn't have any better luck. He got off a single shot, letting it go blind and with no luck, for he had nothing to shoot at. But he was limned against the remaining glow of the fire and a second shot from the far end of the willows knocked him flat. This was the beginning of a deadly bedlam.

The raiders' camp was the apex of a very flat triangle. At each corner of the base of this same triangle were three Rocking A men who had not come this far for the purpose of wasting lead. They had the raiders in a crossfire and they made the most of it.

Curly Garms never got off his heels. He just spun slowly around on them and fell over backward. Whip Thorpe, ever the cruel coward, lunged to stand erect and started to run. In mid-stride a bullet knocked him winding and he came down in a wild tossing sprawl of arms and legs.

Another raider, trying to drop flat to the earth, didn't get there quick enough. A slug smashed his shoulder and he lay, moaning, all semblance of toughness and fight knocked out of him. Another got a smashed leg and he was out of the fight, too. A single raider managed to get back to the center of the willow fringe and was fighting his way through it in a blind, terrified frenzy. No shots followed him, for he was directly in line between the two Rocking A forces.

But Jim Lark jumped up and ran around behind the willows and was waiting for the fellow when he broke through. And with a swinging rifle barrel, Jim clubbed him down.

That was the end of it. It was over almost before it had begun. Seconds only were needed to finish it. But Bruce Martell, as he raced in toward the sputtering fire, knew a certain savage anger that Jason Spelle, the one who had planned all this backlog of misery and cruelty, was not present to share the same roaring fate that had overcome his hirelings.

Carp Bastion, racing up with Martell, yelled harshly: "Clean up, Bruce! We got the flock . . . all but Spelle. Did you hear what was said about Spelle?"

"I heard. And I'll be riding, soon as this is straightened out. I don't know what time Spelle expects to be at the Land Office, but with luck I'll be there waiting. Get that fire brighter."

There was a stack of dried driftwood piled nearby and a couple of armfuls of this on the fire soon had the flames leaping. Then the grim tally began.

Pitch Horgan, Brazos, Whip Thorpe, and Curly Garms were done for. There was a man with a smashed shoulder, another with a leg likewise, and the one Jim Lark had clubbed down, who was still out. This one was tied up and the wounded men brought up to the fire. They were sick and fearful.

"Do what you can for them, Butte," said Bruce. "Couple of you locate their horses. Bring everybody into town. I'll be waiting there for you . . . with Spelle, if I have any luck." He leaned over one of the wounded renegades. "Was that the truth, what was said just before the fireworks started . . . that Spelle intends to rob the Land Office safe in Starlight tonight?"

The renegade nodded. "That's right."

"This the whole gang . . . excepting Spelle?" pressed Bruce. "Any guards out, east of here?"

"No guards out," was the mumbled, pain-twisted answer. "The whole gang . . . exceptin' Spelle." The wounded renegade broke into a spasm of cursing. "Spelle . . . he would get away."

"That's where you're wrong," said Bruce. "He hasn't . . . yet."

He turned to Butte and Carp and the others. "You boys know what to do. I'll send Wilcox in with the horses. Me, I'm going to see how much run that big black of mine has really got in it."

"Mebbe two would be better than one, Bruce," suggested Carp anxiously.

"Not for this chore," replied Bruce grimly. "Spelle and me . . . I've felt from the first that it was written in the book. I'll be waiting for you."

He hurried away into the dark, slipped and slid and floundered through the tricky blackness beside the rumbling narrows of the river. He sent a call ahead of him to tell Card Wilcox who it was coming in. Card was fairly dancing with impatience and uncertainty.

"Sounded like a battle for a little there," said Card. "What luck, Bruce?"

"Good. We collected all but Spelle and I'm on my way to pick him up in Starlight."

"Our boys . . . they all right?"

"Not a scratch. Take the horses in. You'll have to move 'em one at a time through the narrows, but you can make it. See you later, cowboy."

Then Bruce was up and riding. He pounded along the bench land, watching the run of the rim against the stars. When he came to the break they'd dropped down through, he set the black to the steep climb up the talus slide. The black poured willing strength into the climb, forehoofs reaching and clawing, hind hoofs driving, and haunches gathering and bunching powerfully. The final twenty feet were the worst, but the black made it and, with a snort of relief, jammed ahead across the tumbled badlands.

Bruce held the willing animal back. This was no place to try and make speed. Horse and rider or both could easily be crippled in this rough and crazy tangle. If that should happen, then Jason Spelle would still be riding high. So Bruce chased the stars and dodged the shadows and the black told him with a relieved snort when the worst was behind and open, rolling prairie lay ahead.

Bruce leaned over and patted the black's neck. "Now for it, big feller. You've always liked to run. Get your fill of it."

The black did, running with a long, smooth,

reaching stride that was machine-like. Bruce rode high and easy in the saddle, helping the animal all he could. He kept his thoughts ahead, pushing away as best he could the grim picture of gunfire lancing and men dying violently about a guttering fire. It was a picture that would come back to him plenty of times in the future. Yet it was something that had to be done. The renegades had had their chance and would have it no other way. And because of it, settler families like the Carlings would sleep with peace and security in the future.

The night air bored into Bruce's face, chill and penetrating, but it was the kind of rich and vital air a horse could run on, and the rhythm of the black's speeding hoofs never faltered or broke, except at the times when Bruce pulled the willing animal down for a jogging mile before letting it loose for more of that driving, ground-eating stride.

Ahead, settler fires lifted out of the dark, and Bruce dodged them at the best distance he could. Even so, when he passed one, a rifle snarled and a bullet snapped by overhead. Some alert and belligerent settler was taking no chances. The warning was to stay wide, and Bruce stayed.

Despite the night's chill, thin rolls of sweat foam had built up along the edges of the saddle blanket by the time the lights of Starlight winked in across the world. And Bruce wondered bleakly if he'd get there in time.

Spelle's way in would have been by the usual trail the renegades used to and from their hide-out camp—east until out of the roughs, and then a wide circle that could come in directly south of town. It was logical to figure this would be so; and the later the hour, the quieter town would be for Spelle to slip in for his call on the safe of the Land Office. And on Cashel Edmunds, so Curly Garms had said. Edmunds was to be written off, because they knew he was a weakling and might give out more than was wise. This double chore, Spelle had selected for himself.

Well, mused Bruce harshly, that was an angle the renegades should have thought of before. For Edmunds was already taken care of and he'd already talked. As for the Land Office safe, there might be money in that and there might not. Maybe Pat Donovan and Sam Otten and Pete Martin had taken care of that, too. They were solid, honest men and would know what to do.

Bruce brought the black in over the last mile slowly, letting the animal cool out gradually from that hard run. And when he stopped finally, it was at the corral in back of Donovan's store. He tied the black and moved carefully up alongside the store to the street. There were a few lights here and there, in The Frontier, up at the hotel, and there was one in the store.

Bruce's first thought was to go into the store, to see Pat Donovan and find out what had been done with Edmunds. Then he hesitated. For all he knew, Spelle might already be in town, prowling the darker shadows, watching and waiting for the last life to drift off the street before making his try at the Land Office. If this were so, there was no telling what significance he might read in the sight of Bruce dropping in on Donovan at this hour of the night. He might get wary and drift out and on returning to the renegade hangout find full evidence of what had happened and so ride far beyond reach. Even if he bumped into Carp and the rest of the boys, he would still have the night to race away into and throw them off the trail. So, Bruce concluded finally, it was better to wait this thing out.

But he had to get closer to the Land Office. So he went back and around until he came up to the rear of this place. Both front office and back room were dark and silent. Finding a black pocket from which he could watch the front of the place, Bruce settled down to the wait.

Instinctive habit made him reach for his smoking materials, and he had a cigarette half built before he realized this wouldn't do. He crumpled the cigarette in his fingers and let the fragments sift away.

He wished he had news of Brink Carling's condition. He wondered how Hack Asbell had made out, if he'd been able to move Carling to some sort of shelter. As he thought about how it had been when he had carried Tracy Carling into Hack's cabin up at headquarters, a swift warmth swept through him. Old Hack was all right—the pure quill. He had taken Tracy in his arms and comforted her like she was a little child of his own. Tough and crusty and grim as he might be on the surface, Hack had a big warm heart, once he chose to open it. And he had opened it to that grief-racked, terrified settler girl. Yeah, Hack would do to take along.

There was another angle that carried a big measure of satisfaction. In her grief and terror, Tracy Carling had turned to the Rocking A for help, which, boiled down, meant that she had turned to him, Bruce Martell.

A couple of settlers came out of The Frontier, climbed into the spring wagon tied in front, and went spinning out of town. It had been the last rig on the street and its departure held a significance. It was as though the town were empty, now, and could close up for the night.

The light in the hotel went out. Soon after, Pat Donovan's store went dark. Only the light in The Frontier hung on. A wind came in across the miles from the Lodestones to take over full occupancy of the street. It brought a sense of movement, but no sound. Bruce pulled his neck deeper into his collar against the chill.

Indecision began to gnaw. Maybe Spelle had hit town, done his shady business, and gone again by this time. Maybe something had warned him off. Maybe. . . .

Bruce stiffened. Against the dark blur of the front of the Land Office there was movement, solid movement. There had been no sound and all had been quiet there just a moment ago. But now . . . Bruce came to his feet in a slow, careful lift. He slid his belt gun out of the holster. Then he waited. He had to be sure about this. The old, singing chill swept through him, a chill that was at the same time a strange, thin heat. It had always been this way in the flint-hard moments before gunsmoke would roll.

There was the sound of muffled fumbling at the Land Office door. Then movement again, scuffing around as though to go down the side of the place toward a window. Bruce moved forward, two full long strides, and voiced his challenge.

"Spelle! This way!"

Came the droning, explosive curse of surprise. "Martell, by God!"

Strange, indeed, the instinctive recognition that was here. Through the waiting darkness it flowed like a current, direct, bitter, beyond mistake. Behind it lay the machinations of an inscrutable destiny, which moved men through life, laid out the trails they must follow, cast them one against the other at a time and place of its own choosing. And this was the time, this was the place. It was something that had been written in the book, long ago.

Bruce flung further words, waiting. "You're through, Spelle. I just came from Loco Mono Creek. Rocking A was with me. Your gang is wiped out. And now . . . you."

Bruce dropped to a knee as he spoke. A split second later Spelle's gun flamed, and the report of it was a hollow coughing blast across the night. Again and again that stabbing gun flame, and the hard, rolling thunder of its voice. And it placed the indistinct figure behind it.

Old and wise in this sort of deadly business, Bruce had waited for this. Spelle, he knew, was shooting at his voice, and a voice in the dark was a shifty target at best. But gun flame was a positive thing and the man who threw it had to be behind it. So now, with his target precisely placed, Bruce shot twice. And knew that he had hit, both times.

He heard the thin, indrawn gasp of a man hard hit, heard the muffled slithering of his fall, and the thump of the earth taking him.

Bruce went forward, conscious of none of the stir of alarm that was beginning to run through the aroused town. For all his concentration was pointed at what lay in front of him. He came up to the spot, scratched a match, and held it low. The match flickered out and Bruce straightened up, knowing the let-down from a high, bright tension. This trail was ended.

Chapter Twenty-One

The light was on again in Pat Donovan's store. Midnight was well past and the slow cold hours of the early morning were running their course. Sam Otten and Pete Martin, roused in their camps by a messenger Pat Donovan had sent, had arrived but a few minutes ago. Bruce Martell, held in the mood of a grim, dark taciturnity, perched on one end of Donovan's counter, smoking endless cigarettes. Otten and Martin and Donovan gathered quietly a little apart, subdued, saying little.

An hour before dawn came the sound Bruce was waiting for. The muffled tempo of many hoofs. He went out onto the store porch. Carp Bastion said from the dark: "Here's everything, Bruce. The whole kit and caboodle."

They moved to the grim work. Mostly they laid stiffened figures in a row on the porch. Two wounded men were brought inside, laid on the floor. A renegade with wrists tied stumbled in.

Butte Allen looked at Bruce. "Spelle?" he said.

Bruce nodded.

"Well," said Butte, "that just about does it, I reckon."

Bruce turned to Donovan and Otten and Pete Martin. "You've got Cashel Edmunds locked up in Pat's storeroom. And here are three more who will live. What happens to the four of them is up to the settlers. It's their chore from here on out. We've given you a start in this thing called law and order . . . a rough one, but necessary. You can build from here. See that the story is told just as it was. I guess the boys and I can call it a day now . . . or a night. From now on we've got plenty of ranch business to attend to. Let's ride, gang."

At Button Willow Ford on the river, Bruce turned off. "I'll be along later, boys. Go get some rest."

"And grub!" exclaimed Carp Bastion plaintively. "Great Moses. Am I hungry."

Bruce followed the river and, with dawn breaking, rode into the Clebourne camp. Kip was astir, lighting the fire. He looked at Bruce with surprise. "You ride early, cowboy."

"Or late," answered Bruce, swinging down and spreading his hands against the first heat of the flames. "Been a big night, kid. You can forget Pitch Horgan and his crowd."

Jeff Clebourne, yawning, came up to the fire. Bruce sketched the night's events briefly, then hunkered, still and weary before the flames. Cadence came down from the big wagon where she slept, and heard the story from Kip, who pulled her aside.

"The big fellow did it," murmured Kip. "I knew he would. It's in him to curry the wild ones. But it's left him beaten and dark and bitter inside. Do what you can for him, honey."

For all her slim girlishness, Cadence Clebourne knew deep wisdom. Her smile was bright and quick as she moved up beside Bruce and laid an arm across his shoulders.

"It's always pleasant to have you with us, Bruce."

He reached up and captured her hand. "When is it going to be big brother, youngster?"

She colored warmly. "Not long. As soon as the cabin is done."

"We'll throw a celebration to date time from," Bruce declared. "You make Kip toe the scratch. If he doesn't, yell for me. I'll slap his ears back."

She laughed softly. "I don't think I'll have to. Kip's grand. Now I'll get breakfast."

Warm food and the simple order of this camp were just the things Bruce needed to lift him out of the worst of his moods. When he made ready to leave, just after sunup, Cadence had won a glimmer of his old, slow-breaking smile. Kip walked with him over to his horse.

"I know I don't have to say thanks for Horgan," Kip said gruffly. "If you ever have cause to wonder about the price, there's this you can be sure of. You'll never have cause to worry about me again, big fellah."

Bruce dropped a hand on Kip's shoulder. "I'm certain of that, kid. Last night closed the book."

He climbed the trail to Rocking A headquarters slowly, a big man on a weary black horse. Hack Asbell was stamping around by the corrals.

"Where in Tophet have you been?" demanded Hack testily. "You worry a man to death."

"Just stopped by to say hello to my kid brother," explained Bruce.

"How was I to know that?" growled the old cattleman. "For all I knew, you mighta decided to drift outta Indio Basin, just like you drifted into it. Which is something I got to know. How long you going to work for me?"

"How long do you want me to?"

Hack chewed the stub of a stogie. "From now on," he said bluntly. "This is your home, this ranch. Remember the time you snagged me away from that bunch of crazy sod-busters? Well, I asked you why you bothered to. You gave me a few reasons, but there was another one that you held back. What was it?"

Bruce busied himself, unsaddling, giving no answer for some time. Then he said quietly: "My father was just such another as you. You reminded me of him."

"Humph!" grunted Hack. *"Humph!"* But his old eyes gleamed softly. "It's all settled then. Here you are, here you stay. The boys told me all about last night. Good job . . . damn' good job. Knew you'd do it. Now forget it, son . . . and think of better things. Come along and meet the Carlings . . . all of 'em. Brink, he's making the grade, fine. Missus Carling, well, there's nothing in those fine eyes of hers but what was there when we first

knew her. And Tracy, she's my girl. Ain't been so damned happy and satisfied with life since I don't know when. Turned my cabin over to them folks. First time it ever had anybody worthwhile living in it. Now, come along."

Aunt Lucy met them at the door. She put both hands on Bruce's shoulders and smiled her old sweetness. "It's good to have you back safely, Bruce . . . good! Brink's awake. I know he wants to see you."

Brink Carling was pale and gaunt. But there was no mistaking the quickening vitality in his eyes. Bruce took his hand. "This is the best possible news, Mister Carling. And smooth trails ahead."

Carling murmured: "My thanks for everything, boy."

Tracy Carling, coming in from a back room, said nothing. She just looked at Bruce, then moved softly about some household task. But there had been a depth and mystery in her glance that Bruce couldn't understand.

Leaving the cabin, Bruce said to Hack Asbell: "The loot taken in the raids has been recovered. It was in the pockets of the different members of that gang. The money Brink Carling lost will be returned to him. Pat Donovan and Otten and Pete Martin will take care of all that. Now, me for some sleep. My eyes feel like they'd been burned into my head."

Chapter Twenty-Two

The days ran along. Ranch work fell into its usual groove. Bruce stuck to the limits of Rocking A range, but Hack Asbell was in and out of town regularly.

"They like us down there," he told Bruce one evening. "No more cussing and growling and acting like they'd like to tear my ears off every time I meet up with a bunch of them settlers. Donovan and Otten and Martin have done a good job of spreading the real story and proving the truth of things. They had a mass meeting and decided on that feller Edmunds and them other three bad ones you and the boys brought in. Decided to let the government take care of Edmunds. The other ones will get floaters out of the basin when they're able to travel, with the promise of a quick and sure rope around their necks should they ever show in these parts again."

Bruce said: "That's fair enough."

"Hired me a couple of men who know how to finish up the Carling cabin," declared Asbell. "I know Brink and his missus will want to get into their own place as soon as they can. And it'll be damned lonely around this cussed ranch if Tracy goes with 'em."

"Where else would she go?" asked Bruce.

Hack Asbell snorted. "Some ways you're the smartest feller I know, son. Others, you're the most thick-headed." He stamped away.

There were ten days of fall branding to be done, and Bruce lost himself in the driving work of it, yet found keen wine of pleasure in the hard riding, the dust, the smell of the cattle, and the vital worth of it all. And when the chore was done he came out of it loose and cool and cheerful, with all the old shadows gone.

Back at headquarters he found that Brink Carling was well enough to be moved and that the next day he and Aunt Lucy were going down to their old camp with the recently completed cabin waiting for them. Hack Asbell was irascible and gloomy.

"Damn it!" he growled. "I sure hate to see them folks go. Feel like they sorta belong to me, now."

Bruce had not spoken a word to Tracy since his return from the darkest night of his life. And while he made no conscious effort to avoid her, she always managed to avoid him. Now he saw her going into the cook shack, where she was a popular visitor with old Muley, the cook.

Bruce went to the door of the shack and called: "Hey, Muley . . . come here!"

Muley came to the door. "What d'ya want?"

Bruce jerked a commanding thumb. "Scatter!" he mumbled. "Get out of here. Go someplace else."

Muley grinned widely and obliged, limping off to find Hack Asbell. And when he did, the pair of them got their heads together like grizzled and hopeful conspirators.

Bruce went into the cook shack and announced bluntly: "You and I have got to have a talk."

Tracy stood over by Muley's big cooking range. She faced Bruce quietly, hair shining with all its old glory in a beam of pale sunlight lancing through a window.

"You," accused Bruce, "have been dodging me like I was poison. Why?"

She studied him with soft, level eyes. "Maybe I wanted to wait until the grim, dark you had gone, and the happier man came back."

"And has he?" Bruce asked.

She nodded. "Yes. Yes, I think he has. I'm wondering if he's come to stay."

"That is up to you, Tracy."

"Then," she said, a little singing tone in her voice, "he will stay."

Some time later they left the cook shack, hand in hand. And Hack Asbell and Muley, observing from a distance, immediately went into a war dance, beating each other over the shoulders lustily.

Bruce, grinning, pointed to them. "You see, they want you, too. I give you the same words Hack gave to me. This is your home."

About the Author

L. P. Holmes was the author of a number of outstanding Western novels. Born in a snowed-in log cabin in the heart of the Rockies near Breckenridge, Colorado, Holmes moved with his family when very young to northern California and it was there that his father and older brothers built the ranch house where Holmes grew up and where, in later life, he would live again. He published his first story—"The Passing of the Ghost"—in *Action Stories* (9/25). He was paid ½¢ a word and received a check for $40. "Yeah . . . forty bucks," he said later. "Don't laugh. In those far-off days . . . a pair of young parents with a three-year-old son could buy a lot of groceries on forty bucks." He went on to contribute nearly six hundred stories of varying lengths to the magazine market as well as to write numerous Western novels. For many years of his life, Holmes would write in the mornings and spend his afternoons calling on a group of friends in town, among them the blind Western author, Charles H. Snow, who Lew Holmes always called Judge Snow (because he was Napa's Justice of the Peace in 1920–1924) and who frequently makes an appearance in later novels as a local justice in Holmes's imaginary

Western communities. Holmes produced such notable novels as *Somewhere They Die* (1955) for which he received the Spur Award from the Western Writers of America. *The Sunset Trail* (2014), a California riverboat story, marked his most recent appearance. In L. P. Holmes's stories one finds the themes so basic to his Western fiction: the loyalty that unites one man to another, the pride one must take in his work and a job well done, the innate generosity of most of the people who live in Holmes's ambient Western communities, and the vital relationship between a man and a woman in making a better life.

Center Point Large Print
600 Brooks Road / PO Box 1
Thorndike, ME 04986-0001 USA

(207) 568-3717

US & Canada:
1 800 929-9108
www.centerpointlargeprint.com